VIOLENT SKIES

T.J. Lockwood

T.J. LOCKWOOD

MECHA PANDA
PUBLISHING

Cover Art by Nicole Roch and Tiffany John

Second Printing: 2018

Second Soft Cover Edition
ISBN 978-1-7751997-1-7

Mecha Panda Publishing
Coquitlam, British Columbia
www.mechapandapublishing.com

For all the turtles who just wanted to become ninjas when they grew up...

1
THE LOYAL COURIER

THE RAIN IS LIKE SKY BLOOD. Some kid told me that while we were making our way through Utah. Poor thing looked like he'd been alone for a long time, but then again that's where we all are now. Outside of the big cities there's only a handful of us brave enough to dare the mutated wasteland this planet has become. They say we're the unlucky ones. By "they" I mean those still living in the pre-war cities; cities which have been sheltered from the aftermath of mankind's last squabble. They weren't the rich ones or the gifted ones, they were just people who prepared for the worst. They are the people who lived and breathed paranoia. It's a shame really. We all have to start again every time a couple of countries think it's acceptable to pull the trigger on something or someone. The pre-war cities are like tombs and their inhabitants are guards.

"We should head west, you know. It's safer out that way." A strong yet fragile hand grips my shoulder. A man in his late thirties, at least that's what he claims, stands beside me. His name is Jace. He sees the same bullshit I do. I'm sure of it. One doesn't walk across the old highways without seeing a little bit of everything, or rather, a little bit of how everything used to be.

"I don't think it makes a difference whether we go East or West. We're still going to end up hitting an ocean sooner or later." I push the frame of my glasses into the bridge of my nose. They're a little too big, but I can't really go around complaining about it. At least I have glasses.

"Not true, girl. Not true at all." He pulls his hand back. "Ever been to the Oregon coast? Damn that's a beautiful place."

"It's still an ocean." I shrug. "Only went for the odd trip. I prefer the falls myself."

He laughs. "That's all you Canucks talk about: the falls."

"There's nothing wrong with appreciating the falls. It's one of the only places that still looks half decent these days." I pull the strap of my backpack tighter. Inside are only the essentials: a small pot, some canned food and a few knick knacks I picked up along the way. "We should head south when we hit the I-5."

He steps past me with both hands in his pockets now. "You're too honest for your own good."

"I was hired to do a job–"

"And were already paid for it too. Cut and run girl. I'd rather not be hitting up Reno this time of year."

I shrug. "You don't have to come. You are the one tagging along, after all."

He rolls his eyes. "Don't remind me."

And just like that I start walking. It takes a few seconds, but Jace ends up trudging along behind me. Doesn't matter if he's there or not, but the company is nice. Could be awhile before I run into anyone else. Not many people make their way through limbo like we do.

***

"You look like shit, girl." Jace sits across from me on an old picnic table which looks like it's seen better days. "You should get some sleep. I'll keep watch."

That's what I'm afraid of. The headaches aren't going away. If anything, they're getting worse. I close my eyes and rest my forehead into the palm of my hand. "I'm good. Just give me a moment."

"You've been pushing yourself a little rough lately—"

"Jace?"

He nods. "Yeah."

"Shut up."

He just laughs and laughs. Deep down I know he doesn't trust me either. Trust is a sure way of getting yourself killed. Always happens.

"You need some painkillers? Grabbed some awhile back when we made our way through Salt Lake." He talks, but I don't really hear him. My left hand keeps a firm grip on the hunting knife in my pocket. "Girl?"

I shake my head.

He takes the hint.

The air is brisk. The camp fire between Jace and I is just enough to cut the chill. He pulls a blanket out of his pack and rolls it out on the ground in front of him.

"You know I'd rather call you something other than 'girl'. Seems so impersonal."

I lean back, fingers still cradling my head. "Names aren't necessary."

He shrugs. "You know, I told you mine–"

"Doesn't mean I'll do the same."

He stops for a moment. I can feel his eyes on me. A whole bunch of red flags go up in the back of my throbbing mind. My hand comes out of my pocket. The knife follows.

"Well I'm going to call you something else. I'm not the impersonal type." He pauses. "Wallflower."

I look up. "What?"

He goes back to spreading out his blanket. "Your shirt. It says Wallflower. That's what I'm going to call you."

I roll my eyes. "Yeah whatever. You do that."

He lays down and stares up at the stars. My hand relaxes. The knife falls to the ground.

***

I've seen hell before. It comes in the form of scalpels and test tubes. Doctors are the demons and angels; they just don't exist. Life isn't hard it's just complicated. That's just because people are unpredictable. Especially here outside of Reno. I'm told this place used to be as lively as Vegas back in the day. It wasn't exactly the city of sin but it came pretty close. There's something about indulging in too many pleasures that turns me off places like this.

Reno is one of the few pre-war cities which never closed its doors to the outside world. You don't need to pass through quarantine to enter. That suits me just fine. I won't be here that long anyway. Get in, drop off the package, and get out. Easy and efficient. There's never any trouble where efficiency is concerned.

"I'm going to pop in here for a little while. How long you going to be?" Jace reaches into his pocket and pulls out a crumpled pack of cigarettes.

"Just long enough to find this address and get out of here."

He strikes a match and holds it up to the cigarette between his lips. "Maybe we should spend the night. What do you think? It's already near sundown."

"I thought you didn't like Reno this time of year?" I take several steps as the wind hits my face. No, not just the wind. Sand as well.

"Maybe, but I just realized there's a few things in town that I've missed in the last little while." His eyes travel to the girls loitering outside the doors to some of the rebuilt casinos. The message is clear. I don't really give a shit what he does. "These lights, you know, used to be bigger and brighter than anything. Well not bigger than Vegas, but pretty damn close."

"Feeling nostalgic?"

Jace breathes in the fumes and then gently releases the smoke from his lungs. "I was probably around your age last time I was here." He pauses. "God I'm old."

I can't help but smirk. "Age doesn't mean anything, Jace."

He laughs. "Then why the hell haven't you shacked up with me yet?"

"Because." I don't make eye contact. "You aren't nearly pretty enough for me to even consider it."

His laughter continues to echo behind me as I walk in one direction and he goes in the other. "I'll be in the El Dorado."

I sigh. Of course, he will be.

***

My dad always said to count to ten when you're angry. He insisted that it was better to tackle a situation with a clear mind not a pissed off one. Rationality and civility are the fundamentals of negotiation and survival. I hated when that man was right, and he always was. Even now. There's a hat sitting crumpled in the corner of the room. It's too dark to see, but there's something splattered on its rim. My instincts know exactly what it is, but my mind just won't accept it. Without warning I'm thrust forward until I'm inches from this guy's face. This guy with the dirty mustache and the horrid smell of tobacco and Listerine.

He stands in front of me, hands gripping my collar, as if I have something to tell him. I don't. I never did. The message has already been delivered. My job is done. I don't deal in spoken words. Just written ones.

"What did you just say?" He twists his wrists, further tightening his grip.

I wince as he pushes my back against the wall. "That is all I was given."

"How can that be all?" His knuckles are digging into my collar.

"Sir, I was hired to deliver a package—"

"This is not a package." He lets go with his right hand and picks up a crumpled piece of paper from the table beside him. "This is a declaration of war!" He throws me to the ground behind him. For the first time since walking in I notice just how dirty this place is. "You better not be lying to me, girl. I'll cut your tongue out."

War? I push off the concrete and brush the dust off my knees. Too much hyperbole for my taste.

"Look." There isn't so much as a window near me. Two men stand near the door, arms crossed, watching my every move. I need to choose my words carefully. I've never been good at censoring myself. "I'm a courier—"

"You think I care?"

Well that didn't work.

He steps under a hanging light and reaches under his jacket. The crumpled paper falls to the ground. There are several ways for this to play out. My mind kicks into gear.

"Do you know who I am, Courier?"

I do. "I didn't think to ask."

"That was your first mistake." The light shines off the barrel of the revolver in his hand. It is an antique as far as today's weapons are concerned.

One of the men at the door lights a cigarette and exits down the hall. The other one leans back against the door frame and pulls his phone out of his pocket. My attention returns in time to feel his weapon hitting me across the face. I fall into the table to my left.

"Look at me when I'm talking to you."

The taste of metal starts seeping between my teeth. I push myself up slowly. Red drips from my cheek to the table. That's not the first time I've ever been hit, but it still hurt just the same. The air has gotten stale. The lingering scent of tobacco isn't helping. This man is making it very hard to stay calm and collected.

"I'm a courier. The package assigned to me has been delivered. I'm going to go now. Any business you have with my employer is between you and him."

"That, my dear, is where you're wrong." He takes a step to the left. "Just you coming here is an insult to both me and my family."

Family? Of course. It always comes down to family, but the truth is I don't care about things like that. "Then I apologize."

He laughs. "You apologize? You think it's that simple?"

I nod and wipe the blood from my cheek. "My life is run on simplicity. Take this over there and bring this back. Return before dark and you get a bonus. Simple. Easy–"

"But it isn't that easy, is it? Nothing is ever that easy. Apologies, for example, may be easy to say but it's hard to make someone believe." He steps closer and brushes the barrel of his gun beneath my chin. "And sadly, I don't believe you."

Breathe. I need to stay in control.

He steps back. I can see what he's going to do. The gun in his hand doesn't look heavy. There won't be any moments of hesitation. He's going to kill me. His patience is gone. I take a deep breath and follow his step back with a step forward. His gun is raised, but he hasn't had time to aim. My hand is on the barrel diverting the line of fire before he has a chance to fully comprehend what is happening. The man by the door barely looks up as I tear the gun from my attacker's hand.

I squeeze the trigger once.

A phone shatters against concrete.

"You think you can get away with this?" For a second there is silence, but it is quickly interrupted by the loud pattering of frantic steps. Another man emerges through the door.

One more bullet flies.

One more body falls.

"Messy." I flip out the cylinder and empty both the remaining bullets and spent casings onto the ground. "I'm not a fan of these." I toss the weapon aside. "But I'm not afraid to use them when necessary."

He stares at me as if I had shot him and not the other two. It's as if he's wondering about something heavy. He's lost in thought. I can see it in his eyes. "A courier?"

"I'm the best courier."

He shakes his head. "Bullshit." I start walking towards the door. He makes a move for the gun then fumbles around with the bullets on the ground.

I stop. My head starts throbbing. "You're making it really hard for me to walk away."

He gets one bullet into the cylinder. "You think you can—"

My boot connects with his jaw. Metal slides across concrete and I find myself standing over a man with my fists clenched.

This isn't the first time.

I kick him again.

And I know it won't be the last.

My head is pounding, but I don't stop. I can't stop. Tears. I can't stop those either. I don't know how long I'm lost in the moments, but when I finally do pause the room seems fit enough to tell a story. No more. Just no more. My job was done. Why did I stay? Why did I let him keep me?

The door. I walk towards it slowly. My watch beeps. One message appears on its face. 'Is it done?'

I sigh. Of course, it is.

***

I find myself sitting against the side of a building with my elbow draped over my right knee. Breathe, calm down, and remember where you are. This is Reno and it's become way too dangerous for me to stay here. I need to move on. The pounding in my head has slowed to an occasional pulse. Still hurts like hell though.

A metal door crashes open to my left. It's dark, but I can still make out two people rushing out with their tongues down each other's throats. Beautiful. There's only thousands of hotel rooms in the city, but let's choose the alley because that's what's really sexy. I push myself to stand. A bottle topples over.

Both of them stop. It gets really quiet.

"Don't let me ruin your night of passion." I start walking.

"Wallflower?" Jace? I don't look back. I'm sure only disturbing images would be burned into my mind if I did. "What the hell are you doing out here?"

I stop. "I could ask you the same question, but I really don't want to know."

The sounds of frantic movement and a whispered 'sorry' precede the heavy steps behind me. I start walking and before I know it Jace is keeping pace on my left.

"You all done?"

I still don't look over. "Yeah. You?"

He chuckles. "I could have used a couple more minutes."

"I bet."

The neon paints a picture I've never seen before. It's a rainbow of broken colours. I take a deep breath as my watch beeps. I don't have to look at it. I know what it'll say.

"So where are we going?" Jace throws his bag over his shoulder.

I quickly realized I've left mine. Doesn't matter. "Vancouver."

He pauses. "You mean the Vancouver in Washington, right?"

"No." I wince. My headache returns. "I've got another job."

For the longest time he's just following. No smart ass remarks. No whining about the travel time. Nothing. When I do look over all I see are bright blue eyes staring at me. "That's one hell of a journey, girl."

I watch as he pulls out a cigarette. "You don't have to come with me."

He shrugs. "I kind of like you. Besides I'm not doing much else anyway." I take the cigarette from him and put it in my mouth. Instead of saying anything he hands me his match book. "And you've got me curious."

The light of my watch continues to glow. Jace lights his own cigarette as I read it.

'Have you secured the package?'

I look to Jace.

Yes. Yes, I have.

2
THE MODERN GANGSTER

THREE WOMEN WAIT TO DIE at a gas station just east of the I-5. No, I've never spoken to them nor have I met them, but I can read body language fairly well. It's all in the posture; the hunched shoulders, the endless stare at the ground. These women aren't thinking, they're contemplating. I've seen this before. Not them, no I've never seen them, but I have seen the edge of the cliff they're standing over. It's their eyes. They give it away; the impossible choice. People lose hope when they come to the realization that wandering like a nomad reaps little reward especially for those who don't have an endgame in mind. It's both sad and enlightening. None of them see us; not really. Even though Jace and I pass right by. One of them sits hunched with her head resting against her knee, another stands propped up next to the broken vending machine. The last stays leaned up against the building with her hands in her pockets. A rusty revolver lay between them. I wonder if there are bullets in the cylinder. If there weren't I'd imagine they'd be trying to find some.

"I didn't take you for the religious type,

Wallflower." Jace presses the end of his cigarette into his boot. "You've been holding that book tighter than a kid holds their teddy. I don't like it."

I look up just long enough to make brief eye contact. "It isn't the bible, Jace."

He smiles and tosses the end of his cigarette. "Could have fooled me, girl."

It isn't. The book in my hand has passed through many cities. The leather cover is cracked and weathered beyond its age. It is insignificant to most people. Every job I have ever taken is documented within its pages. You could say it was my diary, just without all the sappy details.

"I don't think I'm understanding our route, Wallflower. Why did we slide off the highway again?"

I sigh. "Because you're the one complaining about our food situation. Or have you forgotten?"

He shrugs. "Oh, that's right. Well, a man has got to eat."

"And we've slid off track to resupply and accommodate the pickiest eater of our little troupe."

He smiles. "I know, I'm just playing."

If there is a god, let it be known that I'm going to kill this man if he doesn't stop wasting my time with useless conversation.

"Woah, hey there. We missed a gas station."

I sigh. "No, we didn't miss it. It's just not somewhere I want to stop."

He turns. "What if there's beef jerky in there? Haven't had that in ages."

"It looks scummy. I don't like it."

Jace slows a little until his steps come to a complete halt. I have no choice but to do the same or else I'd start leaving him behind. "Those girls look lonely. We should say hi. You know, to be polite and all."

I shake my head. "You just want to stop so you can ask if they'll fuck you."

"Such vulgar language, Wallflower. I'd never say anything like that."

"No?"

He tips his hat. "No. You want to do some role playing? I'll show you—"

"Ha, you're funny."

"Wallflower, they're just some girls—"

"Who don't look like they want to be disturbed."

There is a moment, between the end of an old cigarette and the beginning of a new one, where he merely shrugs. "You can't tell me what to do, you know."

"I can suggest."

Jace pauses and takes his cigarette out of his mouth. You'd have thought I'd slapped him. "Doesn't mean I'm going to listen." He takes one last drag and then discards the burning roll of tobacco. "We should talk to them."

"What?"

"We should talk to them."

I shake my head. "Why?"

"Because it'll be nice to hear a voice other than yours for once."

"Asshole, they could be murderers."

"Well now that's the beauty of an introduction,

Wallflower. One gets to find out."

If I didn't need to be here I wouldn't be. There are so many other places with jobs that need doing. Why didn't I take them? Stupid. Just stupid. The money is good though. I need to keep reminding myself of this. Jace doesn't look at me as he turns the opposite direction and walks back the way we had just come. The woman with her head against her knee looks up, but only for a moment. There's something new in the air: disgust.

My watch beeps.

I don't look at it.

"Might I interest you ladies in a cigarette?" Jace stands tall and tips the brim of his hat. "They're clean. None of that fake tobacco people are smoking down south."

I roll my eyes and pay little attention to the scene unfolding in front of me. My head hurts. It has ever since we put Reno behind us. The pain is blunt, dull, and constant. It hasn't let me sleep in a couple of days.

"You mean in Texas?" The girl next to the vending machine straightens up and takes a couple of steps forward. Her eyes are bloodshot beneath the mess of oily blond hair. She has the air of an addict all over her.

Jace shrugs and steps to meet her. "Could be in Texas, might just be in New Mexico. Either way, this is just good old American Tobacco."

"Got anything else?" The woman on the ground looks up just enough to make eye contact. "Maybe some Krank or Turbo?"

"Stuff's too hard for me, ladies." Jace sighs. "All

I've got is tobacco and a bottle of whiskey."

"Then what good are you?" The voice is weak, scratchy, and comes from the woman against the building.

My stomach turns. It's all instinct. I don't like this. It's as if I'm waiting for a bomb to go off and I can't do anything to disarm it. Jace takes a step back and glances over in my direction. I wonder if he feels the same way I do. If he does he sure doesn't show it. Either that or he doesn't care.

"Well then it was nice to chat, but I best be going. That's my girl over there. It would be rude to keep her waiting."

"She's not your girl. Doesn't look like she's anyone's girl for that matter." The woman propped up against the wall pushes off and joins the one previously against the vending machine. Jace takes another step back, but the woman moves past her friend until she's only couple of feet away. "So jumpy."

He shakes his head. "Not at all. I just know when it's time to move on."

She shrugs. "All I'm doing is taking you up on the offer."

"The what?"

She smiles and pinches a cigarette from Jace's carton. "The smoke."

Her arm sports a myriad of tattoos.

One stands out.

Jace goes white.

Oh shit.

There is a dance; a tool used to seduce even the most unaccommodating of people. I've seen it. I've done it. It is nothing short of marvelous; a man-made miracle to entrap. This woman is in the midst of her dance. You can smell the cloud of fear engulfing Jace in an irresistible perfume. Does he want her? No. I've never seen him so repulsed. So awkward.

"Do you need a light?" My steps are shallow, but quick.

Jace stares forward.

The woman shrugs. "Depends on who's offering."

My presence has clearly made the other two women uncomfortable. The revolver seems to be getting closer to their reach as the seconds go by. I walk, as I usually do, with my head high and a smirk on my face. Jace tries to make space so I can come between him and the woman sizing him up. I can see the wrinkles dividing her face. I doubt she's old though. Those wrinkles were put there by something outside of the harsh touch of time. I'd bet money on it.

I reach into my pocket and pull out a half empty box of matches. "Does it matter who's offering? For all you know that's a bona fide death stick in your hand."

She shrugs. "All the better."

One strike and red meets an instant bright orange. The warmth of the flame is just enough to cut the slight chill in the air. One deep inhale follows another. Tobacco fills my lungs. It smells sweet like freshly made caramel.

Jace discards his own cigarette and quickly reaches for another.

I'm bathing in the smoke. It's not helping my headache. The throbbing seems to be getting harder and harder. Regardless, it's important that I keep my posture. Too many situations such as this go awry because someone displays any sort of weakness. The matchbook finds its way back into my pocket.

"If it's all the same to you ladies we best be heading off." I pause. The revolver on the ground isn't there anymore. "We've got a long walk ahead of us and this guy doesn't stop complaining every second of the way."

"He seems like the type." It's the woman on the ground who speaks. The revolver sits neatly in her lap. "Damn sexist pigs, they are. Can't stand them. Not in the least. Are you attached to this one?"

I glance over my shoulder. "Just a little. He can be quite entertaining; despite his faults."

A bead of sweat rolls down Jace's cheek. He's recognized what I did a while ago: that he probably shouldn't be talking for the rest of this encounter.

"Does he treat you right?" That one comes from the woman against the wall.

I nod. "If he didn't I would have killed him in his sleep."

The woman on the ground starts laughing uncontrollably. I don't see what's funny. What I said was the truth. Jace chooses this moment to start making distance between himself and the women. I sigh, it's just like him to leave me to finish what he started.

"Well, we best not be keeping you two. Thanks for the smoke, Sugar."

The woman in front of me turns away. I take this as my cue to do the same. There's still the revolver, but it doesn't worry me. There aren't any bullets in it. Don't ask me how I know; I just do.

"Wallflower..." He trails off.

I glance at my watch. 'Coordinates.'

Ever the watchful one. We're running a tad later than I had hoped. It hasn't gone unnoticed.

"We should make camp early tonight."

Jace shakes his head. "What? No. We need to get the hell out of here."

I pause. "Not an option."

A hand grasps my shoulder. "You saw those women. They were sharks out for blood. They've got Polluck's marks all over them."

I nod. "Which is why we need to stay close."

"You been smoking something I don't know about, Wallflower?"

"Calm down."

His grip tightens. "How do you expect me to do that? They're probably his girls or something."

"Or maybe they were and aren't anymore. Either way, staying close gives us the opportunity to use them as witnesses if need be. We aren't snooping. We're traveling."

"This is—"

"But if we come across Polluck's gang and we've got no one on our side then we're open season and I don't like having zero options."

"But—"

I push his hand off. "Maybe next time when I say we should just keep going you'll listen."

I've got to admit, seeing Jace scared shitless

amuses me greatly. He's freaking out, but he shouldn't be. I've been in a similar situation like this before. If those three are out here with nothing but an old revolver then Polluck's abandoned them. I didn't make the connection until I saw the tattoos. There were probably more of them, six more, and those poor women were unfortunate enough to not have enough bullets for themselves.

They aren't in any condition to wander around these parts. That gas station is going to be their final resting place. The revolver is just the tombstone.

3

THE ISLANDS IN THE SKY

I WAS SEVEN YEARS OLD when human cities first took to the sky. Leaders all around the world dubbed it a period of innovation. How could they not? It was the beginning of a renaissance; a golden age. Twelve self-run and self-propelling islands rose above the ground on which they were created and looked down upon gravity as if it had no tether. I remember the wonder and the arrogance I felt, even as a child, boarding city number eleven for the very first time. My father said that this was a new beginning, but I'm not sure if he was referencing the city itself or our future upon it. The way he walked into that city; it's as if the ground beneath it never existed.

Mankind was making progress. We had cities floating on their own. Next step was space. We never got there though. Politics got in the way. If there is one thing I've learned it's that politics come second only to money. It was as true then as it is now. Some things never change.

Jace sits across from me with one hand firmly on his hunting knife. His fingers are shaking. There isn't so much as a breeze in the air. He's just afraid.

I suppose it's warranted. Polluck is many things to a whole lot of people. Some of them aren't exactly nice.

"You keep looking over your shoulder like someone's going to jump out at you. You need to relax." My words break the silence, but that's about it.

Jace just stares off into the distance. He heard me, I have no doubt of that, but there are other thoughts occupying his mind. I lean back against my bag and try to get comfortable for the evening.

Several minutes pass before he sits up abruptly and diverts his gaze towards me. It's as if my words from before just hit him now. "Relax? How can I relax? Better yet how can you relax? Polluck's gang will just beat me, but you... They'll probably do worse to you."

I shrug. "No, I don't think so. He'd have to catch me first."

"Do you think this is funny?"

"Not at all. I just prefer to deal with problems as they come. You can't worry about something that isn't an issue yet. Being stressed leads to brash decisions. I don't like that."

He sighs. "We should have just kept going."

I nod. "Yep, but we didn't. And even if we did, would that have changed anything, really? Those women would still have been there and Polluck's gang still might be around. Now we're just aware that those possibilities are on the table."

"Is that supposed to make me feel better?"

"No." I lean back and adjust my glasses. "It's my way of politely saying that you need to chill out."

The fire between us is starting to die down. All I can see are faint outlines of where Jace and his bag are. He's not reaching for any more wood, but then again neither am I. Eventually, no matter what you do, the darkness will come.

There's the shuffling of gravel and then, temporary, uneasy silence. I hear every movement no matter how small. I doubt he'll be doing much sleeping tonight.

***

War is, by far, the messiest thing I've ever taken part in. No, I didn't shoot guns or steal intelligence; I ran messages across borders. Well, unconventional ones. Seems that when the world went to hell people forgot about patriotism and grouped themselves together the best they could. In some ways I feel as if the packages I carried shaped the world somehow. Perhaps that's just me being too full of myself, but it's true. It's hard to ignore the decimation following every place you were as little as a few days before. That sort of coincidence, if that's what it was, does something to you.

Being a courier is one of the most dangerous jobs a person could have. Unlike most, we don't just reside in a bubble. Bubbles don't do shit. We walk across roads into cities both intact and crippled only to witness, in my opinion better than most, the aftermath of just how selfish the world is. Now, I've lived a life of luxury. It's not all it's cracked up to be. Sometimes I think it's worse than being in a settlement. Sure, pre-war cities have most of the old communications and technologies intact, but there's something about creating a family from strangers. In settlements at least, I know someone has my back. I was born here, but I'd hardly say that I have a home. Not a stationary one anyway.

"Sit down, Red. I've got a good one for you." His name is Leo. I always met him in his factory outside of Vancouver.

I distinctly recall the smell of charcoal as the machinery pressed flat sheets of aluminum around us. Leo owned one of the few functional metal molding plants in the west. The others were so run down and unreliable that he held the monopoly on everything from building supplies to bullets.

He was, for all intents and purposes, the man you went to for metal and sold to both pre-war cities and post-ruin settlements alike. I cared very little for this though.

Leo was my handler.

This was where we met.

He always had an adoration for money. So much of it was made under his watchful eye.

"All you need to do is find this guy and bring him to St. Joseph's. That's it." Leo took a deep draw from his cigarette before it found its way beneath his boot.

"St. Joseph's? You know I don't do that."

"Nobody does it."

I nodded. "Exactly–"

He smiled and placed a watch on the table. "That's why you're going to do it. You're the only one who can. No one else in these parts has citizenship."

St. Joseph's, one of the fallen cities, was also referred to as eleven. It plummeted to the ground over a decade ago and started the last great war.

"I doubt it's any good anymore. Nobody goes to St. Joseph's, especially not people like us. Too many germs and potentially harmful pathogens, remember?" I paused just long enough to inspect the image on the screen. "You've got the wrong job, Leo. No one is going to touch this one."

He reached into his pocket and started to pull out a wad of cash. "You say that, but I think you'll have a change of heart."

"You need to lay off the Krank, Leo. I said—"

The whole wad of cash came crashing down on the table and for the first time since the conversation started Leo looked serious; damn serious. I hadn't seen him like that since the first time we met. "You could wipe your ass with that and still have enough for a ticket to paradise if you wanted."

There was a look in his eye that I couldn't ignore. His posture, the atmosphere and even the focus I first had when I walked into that room shifted. He pushed the watch closer to me. "I don't know much about this stuff, Red."

I did though. The moment I touched that watch it lit up like a flashlight. The sensors were probably reacting to the circuits in my hand. "I told myself that I wouldn't go back there."

"The money is good. I made sure."

I paused. "Who's paying?"

"Sheila."

"Fuck." I hated that woman for so many reasons.

"It isn't about her though. I'm thinking more about what you'd do with the paycheck. Wouldn't need to run around for a while."

My head was pounding almost as hard as the presses around us. I don't know if I was caught in a moment of weakness, but after a few moments I looked up from the glowing watch and started to strap it onto my wrist. "What are the details?"

Leo smiled and scooted his chair back. "I knew you'd come around."

***

"I've been thinking, Wallflower." Jace pauses just long enough to zip up his bag. "Maybe we should get off the I-5. It would be safer, don't you think?"

I shake my head. "And longer. You might be out for a leisurely stroll, but I'm not. I've got deadlines to meet."

"So, you keep saying." He stands and reaches into his pocket. "Don't you want to know more though?"

"About what?"

"Your job."

I adjust my glasses and throw my bag over my shoulder. "I only know what I need to. Too much information is dangerous."

Our walking pace has slowed significantly. Jace hasn't taken his hand out of his pocket since we decided to continue our route north. "But... What if not knowing puts you in a bad spot?"

"What?"

"Some people have no problem shooting the

messenger."

I stop. "You don't have to come with me, Jace. I've been saying that from the beginning."

He nods. "Maybe, but something tells me that you want me to."

"Honestly, I couldn't care less."

"You keep telling yourself that, Wallflower, but deep down I think you care just a little." He keeps walking and I find myself following about half a pace back.

I've known men like Jace before. They all come and go like the vagabonds they are. It's hard to tell what they live for. They spout words strategically; careful enough to leave any detail about themselves absent so that no one can track them down after they part ways.

It's brilliant.

I've been traveling with the man for about a month and I know about as much about him as when we first met.

Movement breaks to the left. Within seconds I have my hand on Jace's shoulder and I'm pulling him to the edge of the road. "Wallflower—"

Gunshots rip through the air.

They're loud; gunpowder. We must be near a settlement and someone isn't the least bit happy. I hate being caught out in the open like this. There's nowhere we can go without being seen. As much as I hate to admit it the best thing we can do is just sit tight.

"Where did he go? Thief!" A man in a plaid shirt looks out from the overpass above us. In his hand is an old semi-automatic rifle.

I'm kneeling just in front of Jace.

His hand reaches for my arm and pulls me backwards. "Get back a little."

From this distance I can barely see the logo on his cap; three chevrons.

I pull away from Jace and stand up. "We'll be fine."

He shakes his head. "You're kidding me."

I start rolling up my right sleeve. "He's a ranger. There must be a settlement nearby."

The ranger's line of sight falls to us. He raises his rifle and peers through his scope. I put both my hands in the air and take two steps forward. The chevrons emblazoned on my forearm are completely visible. If he's good with a rifle he should be able to see them.

"Wallflower, what are you doing?"

I glance over my shoulder. "Not now."

The ranger lowers his rifle. "Did you see where he went?"

He's looking directly at me. I take a deep breath. "No, just movement to our left."

"Shit." And with that he backs up and disappears.

Jace pushes off the ground and walks to my side. His eyes are glued to the tattoo on my arm. What should I tell him? The truth doesn't seem practical for the time being. "You going to keep staring?"

He shrugs. "You're just full of surprises aren't you, Wallflower?"

"I've had my fair share of adventures, Jace."

"You should tell me about them some time."

No, I don't think so. There are boundaries I'm

not willing to cross; especially not with him. There's a settlement nearby so it would probably be best to find it and stock up on supplies.

I haven't been out this way in a long time. I'm sure many things have changed. Regardless, the rules probably haven't. Respect the ranks and go forward as soldiers do.

Now I just need to think up a lie to tell Jace.

4
THE CAPTAIN'S JETSAM

THEY CALL HIM THE CAPTAIN. From what the men have told me, he's been a pilot for most of his life. His eyes tell a story that no one can truly understand unless they were there to witness it themselves. I was on St. Joseph's when it fell. This man watched it happen from the cockpit of his plane. That's what he told me last night with a drink in his hand. I didn't ask if he was one of the men who fired missiles at the propulsion shafts. Doesn't matter. We all have stories and paths which lead us here. What happened happened. Maybe he did, maybe he didn't. For all I know the Captain is just a lying old man. I don't think so, but he could be.

The punch is coming. I can tell by how he stands: hips loaded and ready to spring forward. All his weight is on his back leg. One strong right, then probably a follow up left will be on the hunt soon. I need to be careful. Getting hit, even once, by someone this size will no doubt leave me seeing stars. There is a crowd forming. This man and I have now just become a spectacle. We're little better than two animals in a cage.

He motions forward, but I'm moving before his foot touches the ground. My left arm redirects the strike while my right unleashes an elbow to his face. There is a moment when I'm sure he sees stars, but the game isn't over with just a hit. He staggers and spits out the small reservoir of blood bathing his tongue. There's nothing worse than the taste of metal swishing in your mouth.

I move.

So, does he.

My back slams into the building behind me. His hand is on my throat within seconds. He doesn't apply pressure. At least not right away. Our eyes meet for a long second until my foot smashes into his shin. He winces just enough to displace his hand. I use the wall and push all my weight forward. He falls, and I end up on top with a fist raised.

"Damn." He smiles and lets out a shallow sigh. "You're tougher than you look, girl. But I still got you."

He bridges his hips and before I know it I'm flying off. Despite being on top my position was weak, and he was quick to capitalize. The ground is harder than I remember it ever being. Sweat drips down the side of my face as I roll and recover my footing. The crowd around us has grown significantly. A man in a green hat is collecting bets.

"You sure know how to make a lady feel welcome in these parts." I take a moment to brush myself off. "I just feel so loved."

"That's good, darling. Nothing makes me happier."

He reminds me of someone; someone I haven't

thought about in a long time.

I had forgotten what it was like to just beat down for no reason. I imagine that each punch I land lowers this giant bar of frustration that seems to have climbed higher than I should have allowed it to. What can I say? Jace tests my patience. It's not that he's a bad guy, I suppose I have no way to tell that for sure, he just pushes buttons I didn't know I had.

A kick lands on my inner thigh. I wince, but only slightly. It is, however, something that does not go unnoticed by my sparring partner. His eyes light up. The shark has just tasted blood. He follows up with strike after strike until my back hits something solid, but avoidable. A lamppost? Maybe. No, a mailbox.

Shit.

His fist kisses my cheek a little too hard for my liking.

I fall.

He towers over me like a giant.

"What the fuck are you doing?" Jace springs out of the crowd, but I'm not sure what direction he comes from.

The man standing over me falls backwards. Jace is on him in seconds. The fists rain down, but only two lands. Three guys from the crowd pull him off. I'm sitting up and moving to intercept in seconds. My vision is a tad blurry, but I don't think anyone can tell.

He sees me coming and pulls away from the guys escorting him back. "Wallflower, are you—"

I hit him, rather hard, in the shoulder. "What

the hell was that for? You're going to get yourself hurt."

He staggers back but quickly regains his footing. "Are you serious? He hit you."

I nod. "And I hit him. So, what?"

He glances over his shoulder. "Real men don't hit women."

"Real men see women as equals. I can take care of myself. Besides, we were sparring that's how this kind of thing—"

"No." His eyes, I've never seen him with that look before. It's as if he's challenging me.

The Captain sits up. I can't remember his name. I'm sure he told me when we first spoke, but it doesn't matter. This settlement is run by rangers. They go by ranks anyway. Names are trivial. Earn your stripes and you earn their respect. I've had mine on my arm for years. Jace doesn't have any. This place will always be safe for me, but he should watch himself. I told him that when we first got here.

"Hey, buddy. Let's try this again. You going to hit me? Hit me when I'm ready. That was your freebie." He stands and brushes himself off. "This guy with you, darling?"

I step forward and position myself between the two men. "That he is, Captain. I'm sorry. Sometimes he forgets his place and his manners. He means no harm."

Jace mutters under his breath. "Like hell I don't."

Silence is quickly replaced with whispers from the crowd. Reminds me of the books I used to read about ancient civilizations. Violence will always be a popular spectacle. It was that way back when we built with stone and it certainly hasn't changed a bit today.

The Captain flies past me towards Jace. The crowd chants, but I'm not quite sure who for or what they're saying for that matter. Both men roll, but only one ends up on top. It takes me a moment to recover. By the time I'm finished digesting what has happened the Captain is already stepping off Jace. His knuckles are torn and bloody. The air is cold. I imagine they sting.

"Jace."

My adopted companion lay face down with a rough gash on his cheek. He doesn't move when I turn him over.

"Fuck."

The Captain looks to me before turning to walk away. "Sorry, people are always telling me that I have no control over my temper." One of the crowd passes him a bottle of vodka. "When he wakes up I think it'd be best if you two head on your way."

I nod. "That was the plan."

He takes a large swig of the bottle then pours the contents over his hand. "How far north you going?"

"Vancouver."

"There are three more ranger settlements along this route then. Need anything just stop in. Seattle is going to be a pain in the ass though. We just got word they were on lock down." He tosses me the bottle. "Might be easier to just avoid it all together."

The crowd dissipates. The spectacle is over.

I sigh. "Can't do that. I've got someone there I need to see."

He smiles. "Suit yourself, darling. Good luck getting in though."

"Quarantine?"

He nods.

"Shit."

"More than you can imagine."

He starts walking and I turn back to Jace. Dumbass. He's probably going to complain about this for the rest of the trip. I sigh, roll up my sleeves and pour what's left of the vodka onto his cheek.

***

There are some days when the pounding doesn't stop. It's as if I've got something digging into my brain with a blunt chisel. Not much can be done when I'm like this. Everything bothers me, nothing helps, and it only gets worse if I happen to be near somebody when it's unbearable. That poor soul; I am the first to admit that I can be a real bitch when my head turns against me. Now combine all that with what just happened at the ranger settlement and one can only imagine what's going to happen next.

"You sure know how to pick the rest stops, Wallflower. What the fuck you trying to do anyway? Show me how tough you are?"

I shake my head. "I would have invited you to watch if that was what I was doing."

"Then what were you doing?"

"It's really none of your business."

We stayed in that settlement a little longer than I had intended. Seems to be the story of my life lately. I've never been this behind on a job, ever. Maybe I'm just getting sentimental. It takes me a bit to get used to travelling with someone else again.

"Chin up, Wallflower. Pretty girls shouldn't go walking around with a frown on their faces." Jace doesn't know how close I am to stabbing him with my knife.

"I don't have to smile all the time. I'd look like a pasty Barbie doll if I did."

He shakes his head. "Nonsense. You'd look like one of those models from back in the day."

"Stop."

"I'm just telling the truth—"

"No, you're not you're just—"

He smiles. "Just what?"

I'm going to blow. That's it. Fuck the money I'm going to just explode and murder him here and now. "Jace."

He stops walking. "Look, girl. I'm not sour about anything I'm just trying to lighten the mood. This trip is taking a lot out of me. I'm pretty sure it's doing the same to you. If you want I won't say another word until we get to Tacoma."

For the first time since we left I'm looking at the bandage on his cheek. I can tell it's still bleeding. In one motion I swing the bag off my shoulder and unzip the top compartment. "If you wouldn't mind."

He nods. "Of course, but you should smile more though. You make me think something is wrong when you don't."

I pull out a fresh bandage and throw it his way. "It's not my fault."

"What?"

"I have a resting bitch face."

He takes a step back. "I'm sorry, what?"

I sigh. "I don't smile all the time. That's just how it is. I'm not angry. I just rest in bitch face."

He starts laughing. "You can't be serious–"

"Jace."

"You want me to stop talking now?"

I nod. "Please."

He starts changing his bandage and I try focusing on something other than my head. It works for a little while, but the pain just keeps coming back. I've almost figured out the rhythm. It's getting a little easier to deal with.

True to his word, Jace remains silent as we keep making our way north. Eventually we see the old highway signs leading up to the Tacoma dome. Even as we enter the deserted city neither one of us speaks. Maybe he's just waiting for me to be the one to break the silence. Not sure. Either way I can't help but feel some gratitude. Maybe I will finish this job without killing him after all.

5

THE MEN AMONG MACHINES

WHEN I WAS A LITTLE GIRL I used to lay on my back and watch the clouds weave through the sky. My senses would overwhelm me. It's as if I were witnessing the creation of art without seeing the artist. On those days I was looking at something beautiful. No, I probably wouldn't have been able to tell you what made it beautiful or even how I knew it was. It just was. That was it.

Seattle is much darker than I remember. I suppose that happens when you run an electric dome around the city. It's always dark on the inside until someone flips the switch. Quarantine is never pretty. Especially if it's because of bio matter of some kind. I don't think that is the case here though. We would have heard about it from one of the settlements. No, if there's a quarantine without any announcement then it's because someone wants to leave who isn't allowed to. That narrows down the field just a little. Doesn't make it any easier to get in though.

Jace has been looking through a broken pair of binoculars for the last few minutes. I'm not sure what it is he's searching for, but it hardly seems worth it. The only way in is through the front door and during a quarantine that means either a rather large bribe or a ton of micro-wiring. I haven't been paid yet, so I'll have to break out the tools.

"So, who are we going to see? I thought we didn't have time for any more stops, Wallflower." He lowers the binoculars. "Doesn't look like anyone wants us stopping in anyway."

I shrug. "Just a good friend. We go way back."

"Must be more than a good friend if we're going to skip through a quarantine."

"Jace, remember that talking thing we discussed?"

He nods. "I fulfilled my end of the bargain. It was a one-time deal."

I sigh and take the binoculars from his hand. "That's unfortunate."

"There are worse things that could happen, Wallflower."

I suppose he's right.

Because of the quarantine the perimeter is empty. Getting up close and personal is not going to be the problem. As we move forward it is clear that the dome has a very fragile power source. The shielding flickers randomly. It doesn't stay down for long, a couple of seconds at most, but I might be able to get in if I can time a jump.

I'd need some acceleration, and gravity just might be the friend I need for that. Maybe I won't have to play with any wiring.

"No way, Wallflower. I know what you're thinking. I'm not down with losing an arm today."

I laugh. "That's only if we don't plan this out right. We'll make it in with all limbs attached."

He shakes his head. "We'd have to jump through in less than two seconds."

"More than doable."

"More than dumb."

I pause. "What are you so afraid of, Jace? Even if something goes wrong we'll be in Seattle. There are doctors there that can play with your genes and attach a new arm."

He stops completely. "You ever gone through that, Wallflower?"

"No, I've never had to—"

"It ain't pretty and there's nothing saying that we'd be able to find one of these doctors before we bled out. It's a quarantine, remember?"

Jace isn't facing me anymore, but I recognize the look on his face. He won't follow me in there if I do it my way and I can't risk that he'll still be waiting for me on the outside of the dome when I'm done.

Looks like I'm back to micro-wiring.

"Fine, it'll just take me longer, but we'll need to find a panel."

He sighs. "All I'm saying is that you can jump through the dome if you want. If I have to stay out here, then that's fine. This place doesn't look overly inviting anyway."

"I'll be awhile."

He shrugs. "Then I'll wander off and you can meet me somewhere. I'm getting hungry anyway. Might stop back at that settlement we passed and see if their cuisine is better than that shit we were eating in Tacoma."

I am not OK with this.

"What if I run through and shut down the dome long enough for you to come inside?"

He pauses. "I don't think so. Sounds like it's more trouble than it's worth."

I sigh. "Fine just sit tight. I'll find the panel."

"Are you really going to miss me that much?" He shakes his head. "I've changed my mind. You just go. Meet up with me when you're done."

Under any other circumstances I would skip this visit and continue with the journey north, but I can't. I need to make this stop. "You're not serious."

Jace steps back and allows a giant grin to surface. "See, I knew you cared. My charms are starting to work. There's no use denying it, Wallflower, you're in love with me."

I roll my eyes. "Love? No, I don't think so."

"And why not."

"Because it's love. Some of us don't get that luxury."

For a long moment neither one of us says anything.

"Maybe you're right. Could be just a stupid dream. I suppose I'm the last one that should have an opinion on that. I don't really care about it. Love is an option not a necessity."

I nod. "Very true, but enough of that. Once I find the box I can have it rewired in a jiffy. Are you coming with me or not?"

"I already told you, Wallflower; it'd probably be easier if you just did whatever you need to. Quarantines are dangerous and instead of having to watch my back you could just focus on yours. I'll just back track and find myself another companion to pass the time with until I see you again."

No.

"Jace." I can't sound too pushy. "We're on a roll here."

"That we are, but this just sounds like such a hassle. Get in, get out, do your thing and pick me up when you're done. I'll be waiting."

He starts walking.

Damn it. It's bad enough that we have to stop, but then I'll have to go back for him. There's no guarantee he'll stay there either. I don't want to start this hunt again.

All I can do is look back to the dome.

I better make this quick.

***

There are people in this world who have never had to show even the slightest hint of ambition to get to where they are today. It's as if they were born into or inherited the position they have by some ancient familial rite.

The city of Seattle is probably the biggest of the cities, next to Vancouver, on this side of the continent that is still relatively in one piece. I come here every two years because it has something I need; something I can't get anywhere else.

In hindsight, I should have planned this better. This city and these people, whether I want to admit it or not, are essential to my survival. They manufacture the one thing keeping my head from exploding.

Took me about half an hour to climb one of the ruined pillars of the old I5 over pass near the edge of the dome. Too much time. Now, however, I must be patient. I've timed the intervals. The dome flickers about every forty seconds. Should be just enough to get in and, hopefully, land on something that isn't too damaging. If I mapped out the area right, then I should land just outside of the downtown market.

My watch beeps twice.

I don't care.

"Here goes nothing."

I realize as soon as I jump that I'm going too fast.

Damn gravity.

The dome flickers. I hear the electrical current reboot as I pass through. The ground meets my left knee faster than any other part of my body. I scream, but only on the initial impact. Tears well up in the corners of my eyes. I don't think anything is broken, but damn that hurt.

The air is thin. I force myself to stand, but putting weight onto my leg is difficult. The sounds of metal steps echo in the distance. This is one hell of a quarantine.

It might as well be martial law.

I take a moment to pause and gather my bearings. I'm behind a building across from the market. The streets are dim. I can hear movement coming from the shadows.

"Who's there?"

A door cracks open just enough to let out a small slit of light. "Why are you outside?" The voice sounds like a child.

I stand as tall as I can and put a hand on my knife. "I'm looking for The Minister."

The door closes, a latch slides, and before I know it the slit of light becomes an open doorway. A small boy stands as a silhouette in the middle. "He's not here."

I nod. "Do you know where he is?"

"Subterráneo."

"Thank you."

I turn to leave, but the boy hurries outside and grabs my hand. "Father says it isn't safe outside. He knows The Minister. Maybe he can help."

"I'm a stranger, kid. Your daddy probably wouldn't like you letting me in without him knowing."

He shakes his head and guides me to the door. "He said that anyone with the mark is OK."

"The mark?"

"Yeah. The funny looking shield."

"Shield? You mean the one on my back? How can you—"

As we step inside everything becomes bright. It takes a moment for my eyes to adjust. The young boy lets go of my hand, steps back, and looks up at me. His eyes are a deep gray. He must be an android.

"You need help."

I shake my head. "I'll be—"

But he's running around the corner before I have a chance to finish my sentence. I start walking in the direction of where the kid went. Each step I take shoots a small burst of pain down my leg. My hand still rests on the handle of my knife.

"Here, sit down." The kid comes running towards me with a chair in his hand.

"You want me to just sit in the hall?"

He nods. "Just wait. My father is coming."

Metal steps echo. My instincts tell me to run, but the kid pulls me down into the chair and places one hand on my knee. "Please. We insist."

6
THE PALADIN AND THE MINISTER

I DON'T LIKE ANDROIDS. In all fairness there aren't many of them around these days. Illegal tech. That, combined with the fact that freedom among their kind is a rarity, leaves many a person to go on living without ever having seen one. They were built to be servants and as such they were programmed to obey without question. I remember hearing about the revolt, but I was nowhere near that battlefield. Rather than destroy the machines right away, many of the world's brightest minds were executed if they so much as hinted at studying in the field of robotics. Destroy the source then kill off what's left. Anything involving artificial intelligence ends up being a touchy sandwich of morals and ethics that no one wants to lay their hands on. This one must have slipped through the cracks. There's no way to tell how old he is. The body is simply a casing after all.

His grip is strong. The footsteps echo at a steady pace. I want to move, but also have the sense to not do it too suddenly. My mind is racing. Each second is an assessment; an optional escape plan. If escape is an option. My knee still isn't in the greatest condition. I suppose I could also fight. Though I won't be as nimble as normal.

"Get your hand off me." I'm reaching for my knife.

The android moves his other hand to my wrist and pins it against my hip. The hilt touches my palm, but I can't draw the blade. "I said just wait. Father is a little slow, but he's coming."

I'm soon reminded that androids are made of heavy metal. Struggling is pointless. A hooded man steps out in front of me. He stands with hunched shoulders but still towers over us just the same. The smell of corroding metal fills the air.

"Are you a knight?" He speaks just above a whisper.

I let go of my knife. The android removes his hand. "No."

He takes another step forward. "My boy tells me you have a shield."

There's no denying that. "I do."

"It's dangerous to carry a mark from a faction you are not a part of."

I sigh. "I was a knight, but not anymore. The constant explosions and dead bodies got to be a bit too much for me."

He lowers his hood. In front of me stands one of the most heavily modified men I have ever seen. A piece of cloth covers the man's eyes. Beneath it is probably a pair of ceramic lenses. They're handy in the dark, but when the circuits corrode, looking into light becomes painful. The metal plates and tubing are hidden beneath his robe. Only a few parts are visible around his neck line. He was probably an armored soldier. It's strange to see one outside of their suit.

"Once a knight always a knight." His words are not untrue. In many parts of the coast I would be hunted if people knew of my previous ties.

"That's what they tell me, but I disagree. Any faction that modifies their principles should be prepared to lose a few members."

"So, you don't care for the resistance?" His body language becomes more rigid. It's as if my reply to this one question will determine how the rest of this conversation plays out.

"I just don't care for terrorism."

The android removes his other hand and steps away from me all together. "Father?"

The tall figure whispers something into his ear and pushes the boy behind him. The atmosphere has changed, but the message is clear. This man wants to talk to me alone. One step casually follows another until he drops awkwardly onto one knee, putting us at eye level. The android's frantic steps soon cease as he disappears around the corner.

"You're scaring my boy."

Risk assessment quickly comes to mind. How fast can he move? "You mean the illegal robot?"

"How dare you?" He reaches to grab my arm and I'm half falling half rolling out of the way in seconds. My knee doesn't take kindly to the impact.

"Touch me and I'll gut you." My knife is in my hand now.

The man laughs and pushes himself to stand. "Not like that you won't. You're crippled just like

I am. Question is where do we go from here? You spit on a shield that I have pledged my life to. I am within my rite to peel it from your skin in the most painful way imaginable."

Fuck.

He's not an armored soldier; he's a paladin.

"Your kind dropped my city from the sky."

A moment passes where all I do is tighten the grip on my blade. His breathing calms, but I'm still expecting him to lunge at any second. "You're from eleven?"

I nod. "And if you are what I think you are then this conversation will end only one way."

Protection comes in many forms. The more allies you have the greater your chance for survival. I learned a long time ago that reputations speak louder than words. I've allowed myself to be marked by many. I belong to so many groups as a convenience for my travels. The ink and sub-dermal implants I have were earned by doing things I am both proud and ashamed of doing. I suppose that's the sacrifice for trying to please everyone.

The shield on my back belongs to a political group that once sought to be elected to power in my city. I was young and easily swayed to the ideals of charismatic people. When they took ownership for the fall of my city I was more than ashamed. So much so that I made the choice to leave and stay away for as long as I could.

"Are we declaring ourselves as enemies?" He's tall, built, and even if I were one hundred percent it'd be hard for me to overpower him.

I lower my knife. "What we are is irrelevant.

I came here to see The Minister not to fight with some old man over past ideals. Your boy brought me into this house. I'll gladly leave it."

"You'll die out there. There's a curfew in effect."

I nod. "What does it matter to you?"

"I see the way you look at me. It doesn't matter though. What I believe in is equality."

"Don't push your misguided ideals on me–"

"Misguided? We could debate that for hours if we wanted."

"Father?" The android steps around the corner holding the hand of someone I recognize instantly.

The paladin bows his head and steps out of the way. "You made it here faster than I thought." The android runs to him. "Thank you, my boy."

His cloak is as black as I remember. The cross hanging over his chest is still the same dull gold. "Minister."

He nods. "I'm glad you two haven't killed each other. Blood is best saved for the battlefield."

***

The underground of Seattle is a city of its own. Reminds me of the days in the slums of Vancouver. You could find anything there if you asked the right people and The Minister is one such person. I know very little about him except that he hails from Central America and keeps his secrets to himself.

"You're much later than usual. I'm surprised you're still standing." This room could pass as a laboratory in a heartbeat. I've sat in this chair many times before. He wraps the strip of rubber around my arm and pushes the needle into my flesh ever so slowly. "Does it hurt?"

I nod. "Of course, it does. What kind of question is that?"

"On a scale of one to ten?"

"Seven."

He empties the contents of the syringe into my arm. "You need to be more careful."

It's the same conversation every time.

He throws me a rag and removes his gloves. I know the drill: place pressure and slap on a band-aid. My mind is still focused on the paladin and his android. Too many memories. I don't even realize how long I've zoned out until I hear the gentle hum of a familiar guitar.

"New strings."

The Minister takes off his glasses and sets them onto the table beside him. "Only the best for my lady."

"That's a lady worth loving."

He strums the guitar several times before looking up again. "That she is. She'll have my heart forever."

I stand and toss the rag aside. "And what about the city? Is she still worth loving too? Takes a lot to push you underground."

He nods. "There's some unwanted visitors in the general area. Dangerous ones at that. Quarantine was the best option. This city always loves me, always needs me, I won't turn my back on her just like I know she won't turn her back on me. I know secrets that many want to keep buried."

"Like the paladin and the android? Their kind would be ripped apart if people—"

"That's the glory of a well-kept secret. You scratch my back and I'll scratch yours." The music continues to play. "But enough about all this. What is the great adventurer up to these days? Better yet where is she headed next now that I've given her two more years of life?"

"Minister, that's none of your business."

He laughs. "If you say so, but one of these years you're going to have a change of heart. I can feel it."

"How do you figure that?"

"One day I'll make it part of our payment agreement."

"And if I refuse?"

"You won't."

I limp towards him. "How can you be so sure?"

He smiles and puts down his guitar. "Because you'll always be dying from the inside out and I will always be the only one who can help you."

I reach into my pocket and drop an envelope onto the table beside him. There are no words about it. It's a standard we've both agreed on. Life is never too expensive when you have a plan. "Thank you, but I think I should be on my way now. I have a package to procure."

He nods. "Should I take a look at your knee?"

I shake my head. "No, I'm out of money anyway. Couldn't pay you even if I wanted to."

"Nonsense. I'll just put it on your tab."

"No. I don't have time for that."

He shrugs. "I'd say that you have an abundance

of it now."

I start gathering myself. "It'll be fine."

"And how do you plan on getting out of the city?"

"I said it would be fine."

He raises his hands in defense. "Alright, suit yourself, but I feel that I should grant you a courtesy before you go."

I slip my jacket over my shoulders. "What's that?"

The man known as The Minister stands up and walks to the cabinet across the room. I watch as he takes a key from his pocket and snaps open a pad lock. Inside are an array of weapons.

"I don't need those."

He ignores me and pulls a pistol from the top shelf and a battery back from the middle one. "I assume you have bullets."

"Of course, I don't have bullets–"

"Then here's a box." All three items make their way onto the table in front of me. "I know you don't like guns, but I'm going to give you this one anyway. What caused this quarantine is dangerous and I'm almost certain you are going to run into him."

"Him?"

The Minister puts the weapon together with little effort. His eyes remain on me the entire time. When he is done, the assembled pistol sits silently between us. "Polluck."

One name.

That is all it takes.

I look down and then up into the eyes of The Minister. He knows every thought running through my mind. All the memories collide together into one rapid slide show. I don't know when I picked up the gun, but I did. It feels like it belongs there.

"You still have time to look at my knee?"

"For you? Of course."

The Minister whispers a prayer as he always does when I am ready to leave him. I don't know what he says. Spanish was never my best language, but he looks at me with the same eyes he had ten years ago. He understands the history that many people don't. It's one thing to run into his gang, but another entirely to run into the man. I take a deep breath and attach a holster for my pistol. Jace, you better be at that settlement when I get there.

7

THE ROAD LONG FORGOTTEN

THERE ARE SOME PLACES I've been that I never want to visit again. It's not that the people were unkind or that the environment was unbearable; it was the atmosphere. Something didn't feel right. I've come to realize that my instincts are seldom wrong. I follow them because every time I didn't, I ended up face down in a pile of shit I don't remember falling into. A lot happens when you travel as much as I do. I don't have the luxury of getting to know people over an extended period of time.

Right now, in a room full of strangers, my instincts are telling me to move on. They stare at me as if I were about to get trigger happy. Their thoughts might as well be screaming loud enough for everyone on the planet to hear. What they don't understand is that the gun holstered on my leg doesn't define me. No matter how useful they may or may not be they will never define me.

"Yeah, he came through here early yesterday. Don't know where he went though." Seems to be the common theme lately. Everyone remembers Jace, but no one has any idea as to where he went. There are only three settlements he could have stopped into and I'm currently searching the second one.

"Not even a direction?"

The man behind the counter takes the towel off his shoulder and begins wiping down plates. "Look, lady. I don't take note of where everyone in here is going. It's none of my business. He came in, ordered a bowl of soup, and then left. As long as people pay for their meal their business is their own."

"Even if it was with someone else's money?" Sometimes you've just got to tell a lie to get the truth from people. "I've been tracking this man for several days. He's a thief. Wouldn't surprise me if he swiped a couple tips off the tables here. Just isn't right to let someone like that roam free without a little penance. That is why I am asking super nicely: do you know where he went?"

The towel stops moving and finds its way back onto his shoulder. "I don't know what you want me to tell you. If I say north would that get you off my property?"

A stubborn man without a single care in the world. Must be nice. I push off the counter and start making my way towards the door. My steps are heavy. The moment I step outside the familiar scent of burning wood fills the air. This settlement is defined by its use of fire. The cloud of smoke drifting overhead would probably alarm some, but there really is no need.

My watch beeps twice. 'Why have you back tracked?'

No, I'm not going to deal with her right now. At least not until I find Jace again. She can just sit tight in her watchtower and wait until I have something useful to tell her. There's no sense alarming someone if there is no need.

"You... you were asking about that guy, right?" A little girl no older than ten sits on the ground near a broken street lamp.

I kneel in front of her. "Yeah. Do you know where he went?"

She nods. "A couple people came into town and pulled him out of Rick's bar."

"Pulled him?"

She nods. "He wasn't too happy to go."

Now this changes everything. "Do you know where they went?"

She stands. "That way, towards the mountains."

The moment she points I see it; the mark on the inside of her bicep. Her information was very convenient, but I was going to let that pass. Now; however, I can't. There are people all around us minding their own business on the street. Now that I'm aware of the situation I realize that I've gained an advantage. It also means that I'm surrounded. There's no doubt about that.

"You live with your parents, kid?"

She nods.

I reach into my pocket and pull out a crumpled bill. "Here's a five. Buy them something pretty."

She smiles, takes it, and runs off down the street.

Using children to steer me in a direction is low. Low even for Polluck, but that's alright. Seems like I have little choice but to continue forward. I'll play this out for a little while. If Polluck wants to play games with me then so be it. I clearly have nothing better to do anyway.

***

The mountains to the east were created from debris when eleven fell to the ground. From the settlements and the main roads, it looks like your good old-fashioned rock. Up close, however, the dull metal finish repels the sun's glare like it isn't the least bit welcome. I'm probably walking into a trap, but there isn't much anyone can do about it. I need Jace to continue this journey with me. I didn't take this job and scour half of the west coast just to let it all go to hell right here.

This road is empty; too empty. I can feel many stares burning into me, but there's no one in sight. All I have is a pistol, a pack full of food, and a strip of cracked pavement leading me to a place I frankly don't want to go. My body moves on autopilot while my brain works on overdrive.

I know this place. It leads to a small city I once settled down in for a short while. There should be scouts, always well camouflaged, and a greeter. There's always a greeter.

"Well, ain't you a sight for sore eyes." There he is. That voice. It comes from above.

To my left stands the remains of an old grocery store and perched on top is a man with a rifle in his hands. I draw and fire without hesitation. He falls forward and lands face up in the dirt. His rifle still rests in his hands.

"Get up, Isaac. I know you're wearing a vest."

His rifle goes off. A sharp pain grazes my ear. I don't falter. My pistol still aims at the man laying down in front of me. "You aren't though." He sits up and smiles bigger than a child about to eat ice cream. "Did you see that? Wasn't even looking."

I nod. "Lucky shot."

He pushes himself to his feet and holds out the rifle. "This here is a beauty: bolt action, light frame and I just got her yesterday."

I holster my pistol and wipe the blood from my ear. "Asshole."

He shakes his head. "Says the one who shot me in the chest."

"Well maybe if you didn't startle me."

"I thought you didn't get startled or am I thinking of someone else."

I pause to wipe the blood from my ear. "You need to just... I mean..." What's wrong with me? I can't seem to formulate a thought. "Ugh... I quit this sentence."

He hits me in the arm and swings his rifle over my shoulder. "Still the same Teresa."

I pause for a moment and suddenly remember where it is I am. I haven't heard anyone say my name in a long time. The same? Really? I don't know about that. I've changed, at least I hope I have. "You know why I'm here, don't you?"

He nods. "I assume it's about that guy we picked up near Seattle."

"Where is he?"

"Polluck hasn't stopped talking about him since he got here. He's got quite the bounty on his head."

"Isaac, I don't care about Polluck. Where is he?"

Silence fills the air for a few moments. It's as if the seriousness of this has just come in and slapped him in the face. "Those are dangerous words around here."

I start walking. "Words only have power if you give it to them. I'm here for Jace, that's all. I need him to come with me."

"You don't want to do that. If you go in you won't come out. Just walk like you did before." This isn't like how it used to be. "Teresa."

I just keep walking.

"Teresa!"

As I step over the ridge Isaac runs in front of me. "Get out of my way."

"You're not listening to me."

I shrug. "If you're not going to help me then step aside."

He sighs. "He's with him."

"Who?"

"Polluck. Said they had business to discuss. I don't pry when the boss says to move along."

There's no doubt in my mind that he knows I'm coming. I suppose our meeting is unavoidable. "Take me to him."

"Ter–"

"That's what he wants. Just do it already."

He pauses for a moment, looks at the ground then forward in the direction I was heading. "Do you still have the mark?"

I nod and touch my left side. "Tattoos don't just disappear, Isaac."

"For all I know you cut it off."

No, I wouldn't go to those extremes. As much as I have done many things that I'm not proud of, my marks are my history. Destroying them would be like denying anything ever happened. Remembering is power. In that moment we start walking together. The road eventually becomes a path and the path eventually leads to a tunnel. I show my mark at the gate with two lights shining in my face.

They don't take my weapon. I see the recognition in their eyes. No one dares touch me and rightly so. Some things haven't been forgotten I see.

"This is where I leave you." Isaac turns away and heads back through the gate. "You take care, Teresa."

I don't say anything. My mind is focused only on what lies ahead. I move forward, through the last stretch of tunnel, and emerge in the heart of a small city I remember leaving behind a long time ago. I recognize the faces, but no names come to mind. It has been so long.

I turn to the closest person, a man in an old beat up leather jacket, and grab him by the collar. Leave an impression with aggression. That was always Polluck's motto. "Where is Jameson?"

He spits in my face and moves to break my grip. "Who the fuck are you?"

I kick him once in the shin and throw him to the ground with ease. I draw and shoot one bullet inches from his crotch. "His wife."

A crowd forms.

If this doesn't get his attention, then nothing will. I don't know how long the scene stands still, but I'm knocked out of the daze by slow clapping. I turn just enough to see a man adjusting his cowboy hat. The mark of this place rests emblazoned on the side of his neck.

"You always have to make an entrance don't you, love." His accent is as thick as I remember. Bloody Aussie. He walks forward and puts a hand over the end of my pistol.

"Careful, I might shoot your hand off." I let him push it down.

He smiles and whispers in my ear. "It's good to see you, darling."

I holster my weapon.

He kisses my cheek then turns to the crowd. "Well get on with your day. There's nothing interesting to see here."

"Jameson—"

"I've missed you, Teresa."

And in that moment, I'm caught in his gaze and can't bring myself to look away. I have to remember the history and the reasons I did what I did, but all that doesn't seem to matter right at this very moment. Jameson Polluck is a dangerous man in more ways than one. This is his territory. I need to be careful, but for whatever reason being careful isn't on my mind at all.

8
THE MAN NAMED
JAMESON POLLUCK

I MET JAMESON POLLUCK many years ago just after eleven plummeted to the ground. I left that city behind. He was there, wounded in the aftermath, covered in ash and crawling through the debris like a ranger caught under heavy fire. There were people after him, but I don't remember why. All I know is that he watched me slit a man's throat and didn't so much as blink when I took his gun out of his holster. I was young, but not innocent. In the end we traveled together from one side of the continent to the other. I would be lying if I said I wasn't happy. It was probably the happiest I ever felt in my life, and after the politics I had just walked away from I needed someone to lean on. He was there, and I had no intention of pushing him away.

"I thought you were still mad at me, darling." He sets two glasses in front of him and pours a small amount of whiskey into each. "Didn't expect to see you again."

I slide a chair out from the small table and take a seat. My hand rests inches from my holster. "I'm still mad at you."

He takes out a third glass and fills it with water. "Then why are you here?"

"It's not because I missed you."

He sighs, takes a sip of whiskey then sets the other two glasses in front of me. "I don't like that."

"It doesn't matter." I look between the two glasses. "What are these for?"

"I thought you could use a drink."

I pause. "I look so thirsty that I need two glasses?"

He shakes his head. "No, but all I have right now is straight whiskey and if I remember correctly you have a difficult time drinking hard liquor without something to chase it with, or am I wrong? All you need to do is tell me."

No, he isn't wrong.

The glass finds its way off the table and before I know it I'm pouring back its contents rather quickly. The alcohol burns the back of my throat just like it always does. I let it sit there until it becomes unbearable. The water helps, but the after taste still lingers.

"You picked up a man named Jace from one of the settlements." I set my glass on the table. "Where is he?"

Polluck pours himself another whiskey then sits down in the seat across from me. "You need to stay away from this one, darling. The man's got a history."

"We all have a history."

"True, but his is longer than yours and mine combined."

I doubt it. "He's my job."

"And where are you taking him?"

I lean back in my seat. "St. Joseph's."

He breaks eye contact and stares past me. It's something I've come to recognize; the prologue before the story. Maybe he's thinking of past times. Despite everything, life used to be pretty damn good. One after another all the cogs just fell into place, but somewhere along the line things got loose.

"Why would you go back there? After everything that has—"

I nod. "This time it's all about the money."

He sits back. "Money? Is that what this is about? If that's what you need then it's yours, darling. Every cent I have. I can always get more. The tributes come in every month—"

"That's dirty money, Jameson. You know how I feel about that."

"All money is dirty. That's the way the world works. I know you think ignorance is bliss but where do you think your paycheck is probably coming from? My money is safe—"

"Safe? I don't think—"

"Safer than you wandering up the coast." He pauses and pours himself another glass of whiskey. "You know I don't like that."

Maybe that's why I do it. There are many things he does that I don't like. It's one of the reasons I left in the first place. When Jameson and I created this place, this gang, it was for protection. Out here there's no shortage of people looking for some. Where we differ is in our ideals. He protects through aggression. I like protecting with the use of words.

"Jameson, look I—"

The door behind him opens. He's turned around and standing before I can blink. A kid no older than sixteen stands in front of us with a piece of paper in his hand. "I'm... I'm sorry for interrupting. It's just... There's a man at the gates. He said to give this to you."

Polluck steps forward, takes the paper, then rips it up without reading it. "Tell whoever it is that they can wait. I'm in the middle of a rather important conversation."

"But..." The kid clears his throat. "He's a ranger."

"Doesn't matter."

I lean forward and look the kid in the eye. "Polluck and I are almost done here. He'll be right out."

He turns. "No, we're not."

I stand, walk to the door, and motion for the kid to leave. "Jameson, whether you like it or not, we are." I let go of the handle. "I'll be leaving with Jace."

He steps forward and wraps his arms around me. "Teresa..."

I look down to the ground. "I can't be around this life, Jameson."

"Are you sleeping with him?"

Blunt as always. "No."

"Do you want to?"

I turn into him. "Stop being jealous. He's not my type."

No words, just one kiss. I think back to the days before all this and then to the days after. So many people got hurt because of the two of us and this place we created. We were no better than the mafia of old. Our tactics were just the same.

What happened to us? It's moments like this that encourage me to forget, but I can't.

Why didn't we just keep wandering the continent like we used to?

We part for a moment. His eyes tell a story I remember all too well. The ending wasn't the least bit happy.

***

I had been wandering on my own for several days doing a job for Leo. It was a simple package drop to a smaller settlement near Lynnwood. I didn't have to do courier work anymore, but I loved it too much to stop. There's just something about the notion of always heading somewhere that kept me going. Besides, no matter how long I was away I always came back home. Polluck was different then or maybe he wasn't. I'm not entirely sure.

"Send Leo, my best. This helps a lot." The woman's name was Lisa. She was only a few inches taller than I and worked the fields with boys. It was a poor settlement, but they got by.

"I won't see him for a while, but I'll let him know the next time we run into each other."

"You heading home?"

I nod. "Yeah, I think it's time."

"Well, send my regards to your husband." She looks down at my ring. "He must be a very confident man if he lets his wife wander the country alone."

She had no idea. Polluck was the epitome of

confidence.

The gunshots started a few moments after.

The settlement became a war zone in mere minutes.

Most of that day became nothing more than a blur of memories. Polluck was there with his men. A lot of people died. The package I was carrying was their payment, a loan from Leo, to be given to Polluck for the protection the gang provided. They were also several months late making this payment.

Somehow, I ended up between Lisa and my husband. The rage in his eyes seemed so clearly directed at me. "Jameson, stop."

And I really think he was going to, all the men were, but when I stepped away from the woman I shielded the click of the pistol in her hand changed everything. I don't know if she was angry at me for knowing the man in front of her or if she was strictly a lousy shot, but that bullet was what split Polluck and I apart. It showed me something I either failed to or didn't want to see.

It tore through me, I hit the ground, and Polluck made sure she got more than a dozen bullets to the head.

I loved him, I still do, but that was one of the days when love didn't mean shit. Polluck shot her down, and I don't blame him for how he reacted, but I do blame him for being the catalyst which pushed someone over the edge.

Whether I wanted to admit it or not the relationship was bad for me. He never hit me, and we never really argued, but the things he did to others made me question myself more than I ever had. Was I that heartless? Could I be that cruel? If I dug deep into my memories, then the answer was undoubtedly yes and that wasn't what I wanted.

So, I left, and he never followed. Maybe it was because he knew there was still love there. Who am I kidding? It was probably because he knew I'd come back. I always did.

"I still love you, darling."

"I know."

He pulls me close.

There's blood on the inside of his collar.

For just a moment I ignore it.

No, love was never the issue. It still isn't. Beneath the scent of whiskey is just a man doing what it is in his nature to do. He can't be changed, and I have no right to try and change him. So, the question is where do I go from here?

"Teresa?"

I pull back just enough to really look at him.

Just one more kiss and then I'll walk away.

9
THE GRACEFUL DEAD

SOMEWHERE DOWN THE LINE I stopped caring about a multitude of things. I don't know what prompted it or why it happened; it just did. For a while it bothered me. Change has never really been my strong area. Don't get me wrong, I'm not afraid to embrace it when it comes. There's just always a bit of an adjustment period when something monolithic comes into the picture, but this was different. I can recall isolated incidents when I'd look into the mirror and criticize my new irregular bouts of arrogance.

When had I become so bold?

When did I start looking down at people no different than myself?

These were the questions which started many hours of reflection. It was as if I was becoming a person I didn't think I'd be able to recognize. I was, for all intents and purposes, going against the path I thought I had set myself out on. I'm a good person. I need people to believe that. I need for me to believe that.

It's still dark outside, the sun hasn't risen, and I find myself waking up alone struggling beneath the sheets on a bed I once knew. This isn't the first time. It starts with a reach. I don't know what I'm expecting to find. All that lingers is the faint scent of whiskey and the fading trail of body heat.

I've gotten too distracted.

It's time to move on.

Two knocks echo from the door. I barely have time to sit up before it opens. "Mr. Polluck, Greg sent me to come and..." She looks up from her clipboard and makes eye contact.

Awkward silence.

I hate awkward silence. "Umm... Hi."

She turns around just as I swing my legs out from under the covers. "Frick, I'm so sorry."

It really doesn't matter. "Do you know where Jace is?"

"Yes, but Mr. Polluck said he was going to be staying with us awhile."

I start collecting my clothes from the various corners of the room. "No, he's going to be leaving with me. We both have a bit of a journey ahead of us."

She's young. Probably no older than twenty, but the way she stands emits a maturity that I haven't seen in a long time. She still doesn't look back at me. Is it out of respect for me or loyalty to Polluck? She doesn't even know me. It must be for him.

I dress, finish fastening my holster and take the safety off the pistol. She moves slightly at the sound of the familiar click. Her stance has changed. I can see the invisible wheels turning in her head. It's all threat assessment now.

"I'm not going to hurt you." I walk up beside her,

pistol still in hand. "I'm just in a bit of a hurry."

She turns slightly. "You're making me uncomfortable."

I flick the safety back on and holster the weapon. "Is that better?"

"No not really." She's fully facing me now; analyzing the situation just as I am. "Mr. Polluck isn't here to authorize a guest for Mr. Marshall."

Mr. Marshall? Is that Jace?

"I don't care what Polluck authorizes. We need to go and you're going to take me there."

The clipboard drops. I barely hear it hit the ground as suddenly one hand finds its way around my collar and the other over top of my weapon. I'm falling back as she rushes me forward towards the table. Instinct takes over. Both my hands rest firmly over hers.

She's strong; stronger than I expected. "Mr. Polluck gave me explicit instructions. He needs to authorize a visit."

Like hell he does. I pivot sideways and force her right hand off my collar. She falls first. I land on top with my knee firmly pressing against her chest. "I can make my way around here without your help. I just asked as a courtesy."

I'm not sure how it happens, but before I can process what's happening I'm rolling off and our positions reverse. "Please just stop."

"Where's Jameson? This is ridiculous."

Within seconds the pressure on my chest is lifted and she stands over me with her hand extended. What the fuck just happened? "I agree so let's go find him."

I shake my head. "Are you kidding me? Get away from me."

She retracts her hand. "Are you OK?"

"No, I'm not. Why would you even ask that?"

"It's just..." She sighs. "Something I was taught a long time ago."

I push myself up off the ground. "You need to stay away from me."

"Well maybe you shouldn't scare people with guns."

This is stupid. It really is. "Just get out of my way."

I move past her towards the door as she reaches down and picks up her clipboard. My mind is reeling. How did she flip me? My steps echo, but so do hers. I glance over my shoulder to see if she's following, but all I see is a skinny short-haired girl walking off in the opposite direction. Could she have killed me? Probably. I don't like that. Not at all.

***

There are moments when even the most stern and effective logic fails to sway those into acting how they should. This is one such time. The people I pass do nothing but stare. It's as if they all know something I don't. Normally I wouldn't care, but this is something different. I can feel it. This settlement was always stern and to the point. When did it get so many secrets? Or maybe what I'm sensing is the overwhelming amount of gossip cycling through people's minds.

I've searched the main buildings with little

guidance. Where is he? Where would Polluck keep his guests? Fuck if I know.

"I just want to know where he is."

The man in front of me isn't budging. I can sense his fear. He probably knows who I am, but isn't acknowledging it. "I don't know. No one questions the boss."

"Well fuck you too." This is useless.

Every person I come across tells me pretty much the same thing.

I pause for a moment and take in my surroundings. This settlement isn't a city. There must be something I'm missing. It's most likely staring right at me I'm just too flustered and pissed off to see it. I need to take a deep breath and calm down.

"I didn't mean any offense, ma'am. It's just that when the boss is where he is none of us want to go anywhere near him."

I turn back. "So, you do know where he is?"

He sighs. "I've got an idea."

"Tell me."

"Are you really his girl?"

That's not something I really thought about in a long time. "If you're worried about what I'll see then don't. I know who he is and what he is capable of."

He pauses for a few moments then looks me in the eye. "He's probably in the storage area below the concourse."

"Thank you."

I waste no time in retracing my steps back to the first building I began my search in. The halls are vacant. They weren't when I first came in here. Basement though; I didn't know there was one.

"He's going to be a few minutes." That voice. "If you just wait here I'll go get him for you."

I turn and see the same girl from this morning. "I'll go to him. Where is he?"

"It's rather bloody in there."

My eyes widen. "Just answer the question."

She motions to the door behind her and I'm moving faster than I had all day. There are stairs, but I don't count them during my descent. The sounds of hard blows echo as I emerge into an open room with a table, a chair and two people.

"Jace."

Polluck turns and faces me. His knuckles are crusted with layers of blood both fresh and dried. "We're almost done here, darling."

I hurry forward and push my husband aside. "What are you doing, Jameson? This is how you treat your guests?"

He shakes his head. "This man was going to kill you. I refuse to let that happen. No lowlife dog is ever going to touch a hair on your head. Don't you do your research on who you take with you on jobs?"

Jace isn't moving. His face has been torn to shreds.

"Because they're worse than you, right?"

You'd have thought I hit him. "That's not funny, darling."

"No, it isn't, but neither is this. Let me finish my job."

Polluck grabs a bottle of water and pours it over

his hands. "This is the only way I know of protecting you, Teresa."

"By being a monster?"

He looks away. "If you really mean that then why did you come back and see me as long as you did? That wasn't part of the job."

A valid question. "No, it wasn't. Whether I want to admit it or not that part was nice, but even so you still disgust me. I've turned a blind eye to a lot of things but using children to deliver your messages, Jameson, that's low even for you."

An uneasy silence fills the air between us.

"Now let him go. We're lea—"

He clenches his fists. "I don't know what you're talking about."

I put my hand on my pistol. "What?"

"That hurts, Teresa. I'd never use children to do anything. You should know that."

He walks towards me and I don't feel as though I'm even breathing. I'm too lost in my thoughts. Of course, it was him. The mark was there. I saw it. He puts a hand on my shoulder and I take mine off my weapon.

That's when Jace opens his eyes and starts struggling against the rope. "Wallflower?"

But I don't move. There are too many variables. This is why I don't like asking questions during jobs. I just finish them and move on. Anything else makes things far too complicated.

10
THE UNLIKELY THREESOME

THERE ARE DAYS WHEN all I can think of are the 'what ifs' and the 'what could have been' in not just my life but in the lives of those around me as well. Back on eleven there were clear skies every day. The whole city reached just high enough over the clouds to surpass any harsh weather and give off the illusion of paradise. I say illusion because that is exactly what it was. My father was too enamored to see past the perfectly white walls of every hallway in every building. I came to hate them; so plain and unoriginal. Humanity lost a little bit when they took to the skies. St. Joseph's is the constant reminder. Everyone has something in their past that they don't want anyone else to know about. It's in the nature of all humans to have at least one or two dark secrets.

The blood lust spills over into every corner of the room. The rage in Polluck's eyes are unprovoked; at least to me. Before I can react, his fist travels the short distance and strikes Jace hard enough to knock him, along with the chair he's tied to, backwards.

"Don't you dare talk to her—"

"Jameson!"

He doesn't look at me. I pull him back as he moves to continue his onslaught. The aggression turns just as he does. One hand grasps my collar as the other prepares to unload a heavy blow. I've already drawn my pistol. The tip of the barrel rests firmly against his abdomen.

"Let go of me." Our eyes meet for a long moment. "Now."

His grip lessens. "Stop telling me what to do, Teresa. It's starting to piss me off."

I click off the safety. "I'll drop you right here."

He leans in and whispers. "No, you won't. We've been through this before, darling."

Jace stirs behind us. I hear it which means Polluck does as well. My thoughts travel. I don't notice the hand on my pistol until it pushes the barrel down. Polluck is the only thing, only entity, I feel now; his grip tightens, his words stab, and blood engulfs him in a cloud of memories I can recall without a second thought. When we fight it's bad, but when things were good they were amazing between us.

Just as I feel a shift in his weight, footsteps echo. "Mr. Polluck."

It's that girl.

"What do you want, Paige? I'm in the middle of something."

She walks over to Jace and kneels over him. "Isaac is outside. Says he needs to talk to you. It's urgent."

Polluck shakes his head. "I doubt it. He's always looking for an excuse to leave his post. Handle it."

"I can't."

Polluck immediately let's go of everything. I stumble backwards as he turns his complete attention to her. "What do you mean you can't?"

"He won't talk to me."

"Well then make him talk. You know how to do that. I know you do."

She pauses then lifts Jace and his chair back up. "He says it's about the ranger who came by yesterday. This needs your attention."

"I said handle it, Paige."

"Mr. Polluck." Her focus turns to me, but only for a brief second. "I said I can't."

He takes one step and all I see is an opportunity. I raise the pistol over my head and slam the end of the grip into the back of his head. He falls face down. Paige runs to his side and checks for a pulse.

"He'll live."

She smiles and inspects the aftermath. "I figured. I'm just checking though."

Her posture and overall demeanor changes. In this moment I make the complete realization that Isaac isn't waiting outside. Even though she hasn't really said anything I can tell that there has been a shift. It's as if she's not the same person I met earlier in the day.

I reach to the back of my belt and pull my hunting knife from its sheath. "Why did you do that?"

"Do what?"

"You know what."

"Because it's my job." She sighs, rolls up both sleeves, and turns Polluck over. "Frick, you made such a mess."

That's when I see it; the stem of lavender on her

wrist.

Fuck.

"Sheila."

She nods. "Yeah, you've got her pretty worried. Apparently, you're rather behind schedule on this job."

I am. "I'll finish it when I finish it."

Paige stares at Polluck for a moment. "I'm sure you will, but I have my own job now, so I think we should get a move on."

I shake my head. "No. I don't care what Sheila told you to do, but it ain't happening if it entails what I think it does."

She shrugs. "Thanks for expressing your opinion, but I'll do as I please. I've exposed myself here. Once Polluck wakes up I won't be welcome here anymore. It's not safe for me to stay."

"Not my problem."

"Didn't say it was."

"I think you and I need to—"

Jace coughs twice before opening his eyes again. "Wallflower?"

I cut the rope binding him to the chair as Paige helps him stand. She looks to me then to Polluck. This is bullshit. I don't need an escort. I can finish this without anyone's help. Both of us grab an arm and help him climb the stairs.

"Well, hello there. Who is this pretty thing?" He looks over to Paige who turns bright red and makes sure not to establish eye contact.

I let him go and let her support all the weight. "Shut it, Jace." I then turn to her. "You got a plan?"

She nods. "Yeah, I thought we just walk out the

front door."

***

Jameson never met Sheila and I never really talked about her with him. She's not someone I normally associate with. I did once, but that was a long time ago. What she is, is a pain in my ass. Every job I do for her always leaves me with an unwanted complication. I run around and do the heavy lifting while she sits tight in one of the old high rises in Vancouver like a queen on a golden throne. It's just like her to keep someone close to Polluck.

Paige, the girl is crazy. One minute she can be blunt and mature, the next she can be reminding me of her age. I don't want her around me or my job, but I don't think I could get rid of her if I tried. The ease in which she flipped me earlier still boggles my mind. There's skill there and it worries me. Means she has training like I do.

"I'm just trying to wrap my head around this, Wallflower. How did you know where I was? How did you get by him?" Jace presses a piece of cloth against his face and tries, ever so slowly, to wipe away the dried blood.

"Used my charms. How did you get yourself caught anyway?"

He chuckles. "So quick to change the subject."

Paige throws a piece of wood on the fire then sits down next to us. "She slept with him."

Jace drops the cloth and tilts his head sideways. "I'm sorry, what? That doesn't sound like our Wallflower here?"

For a moment I'm stunned. "You little shit."

Without warning she bursts out laughing. "Oh man. Holy frick! The look on your face." After a few seconds she clears her throat and directs her attention towards Jace. "I'm just kidding. No, can't you tell? She got herself a gun, knocked some heads, asked for some help, I took pity and here we are. Bam, master escape plan."

He shakes his head. "But that's Polluck's gang we're talking about. No way in hell he's not coming after us."

Paige shrugs. "No, I think we're good for now. We just walked out the front door without so much as a fuss after picking you up. There's respect for the people who stood up to Jameson Polluck."

His eyes widen. "Are you out of your mind? You know what he'll do if he finds us. We should just go. Forget about camp. We need to get the hell out of here fast. Right, Wallflower?" Jace turns towards me.

Paige smiles, shoots me a nod, then continues poking the fire. "Why do you call her Wallflower?"

"That's not important!"

I clear my throat. "Just hold up, you two—"

"No." Jace picks up the cloth and starts scrubbing as fast as he can. "It's not safe."

"I think we need to calm down here." I snag the cloth from his hands, pour some water on it, and hand it back to him. "It's dark and we're fatigued. We can leave first thing in the morning."

Paige shrugs. "Might be a better plan. Then we can get a decent start. What do you think, Jace?"

He just stares into the fire. "I... I don't know."

Paige is cordially packing as Jace freaks out and starts muttering random nonsense. He's fixated on nothing more than upping the pace of our travel. Definitely one of Sheila's. She manipulated him so quickly. I don't know if it's arrogance or confidence I'm seeing, but she knows what she's doing.

Well played, girl. Well played.

11

THE WANDERING CANINE

INSIDE ALL OF US is the will to survive. The degree of which we will go for this survival, however, depends on the decisions we've made. I've never been one to believe in anyone's power other than my own. My father once believed in a god. I never really cared enough to find out which one, but all that seemed to change when we boarded eleven. It's as if that city put us in god's reach. Oh, how humanity thrived in its arrogance. Some things in this world will never change.

"Maybe we should slow down a little, Jace. You're still in rough shape." The man's walking with a limp that just seems to be getting worse every few steps he takes. There's determination there. Either that or I'm witnessing just how stupid a man can be.

"I... I don't care." He sighs. "I've never had a beating that bad in my life. Not even when I was being a little shit."

Paige smiles, but says nothing.

I speed up, put a hand on his shoulder and pull him back. "Jace, I'm serious. You keep going like this and we'll end up carrying you to Vancouver."

Paige shrugs. "Speak for yourself. I'm not agreeing to carry anyone."

He turns and puts his hand on mine. "Wallflower, that man scares the shit out of me."

"Why?" Paige rolls her eyes. "Why do you keep calling her Wallflower? Am I missing something?"

Jace looks as if he's going to break. All the signs are there. I ignore Paige's question and focus on the obvious. "Look." I take a deep breath. "We've got a head start. Everything will be fine, but we need to get you looked at. I'm not a doctor, but I know—"

"I am though. I'll be fine." His skin is cool to the touch. He turns back to the path in front of us and takes a few steps. "I'll survive, Wallflower. At least until we get into Canada. It's not too far."

What? For a single moment nothing else seems to matter. A doctor? Bullshit. I don't press the subject though. This is neither the time nor the place and quite frankly that's more about him than I really wanted to know. Still, there's something different about him now. Maybe it's the tone of his voice or just his posture; but it's enough to make me feel wary. I'm not sure of what though. Paige walks ahead for the first time since joining us. She says nothing. She just carries on. I suppose that's what we'll all be doing whether we like it or not.

***

The Minister once said a prayer for me when I had visited him for the second time. He told me that there would always be forces in this world which challenge all moral compasses to point the way between right and wrong. There had to be a balance. When there isn't one, the world always seems to find a way to correct itself. The fall of eleven was one such event. Will there be more in my lifetime? Probably, but I doubt any would come close to changing the world as much as it already has in the last century. Humans touched the sky then fell to the ground in what I would say was record time. Historians didn't even have the chance to take out their pens.

Now I don't profess to know The Minister even remotely well, but I will admit that there is wisdom to his words. The man has eyes and ears everywhere. He knew I needed his help before I did. When I looked into his eyes for the first time it's as if he could sense my pain. Polluck spoke of him fondly. I didn't realize until much later that he hated his guts. I wish people could just be up front about their feelings.

We finally crossed the border about an hour ago. It used to be a much larger endeavor. National security and all that. Doesn't seem to do much now anyways. Took a while to find a doctor that didn't look like he'd do more damage than good to Jace. This clinic is independent; as far as I can tell anyway.

"You've got bots in your system, don't you?" The question is simple, but is also a little too close to home for my liking. Paige sits back in her seat and starts playing with her watch.

"Did Sheila tell you to ask that?"

She shakes her head. "No, I'm just curious. It's pretty obvious anyway."

I put down my pen and look up from my book. "Oh really?"

She nods. "Your eyes are bright green. Only happens with an overload of technology."

"You don't know what you're talking about."

"I think I do." For a long moment the two of us just stare at each other. She's got this amused look in her eye. It's as if she doesn't really give two fucks about any of this. "Holy frick you need to loosen up."

"I'm really not in the mood to play games."

"I'm not playing any." She pushes a button on her watch then sits up straight. "Bots can't be good for your system. I heard they do more harm than good."

"Is that so?"

"Yeah, but you sound like you know that. Don't last too terribly long either. Two years max. Might as well use nanites instead."

I close my book and stow the pen away in my pocket. "Too expensive."

"Sweet, I was right." She smiles. "Expensive, yes, but at least they'd repair the damage."

"Maybe. Doesn't matter though."

"You get what you pay for."

"I know."

She looks as if she wants to speak, but doesn't. Instead there is a moment when the only sound in this room is the electricity flowing into the lights above us. The hum is faint. Most people don't even realize that it's there. I do though, and so does she.

The door we came in opens and an old man walks in with his dog trailing in behind him. Neither one of us says anything as he takes a seat. He looks rather well off. Probably has property nearby. His suit, however, is tattered just enough to suggest a minor struggle. The jacket is ripped at the elbows.

Paige waves at him.

He doesn't wave back.

"A friend of yours?"

She shakes her head. "No."

"Then why are you—"

"His dog is cute."

Jace emerges from the hall with a few freshly applied bandages and a hand lodged deep in his pocket. "This is why I didn't want to come here. Guy charges a fortune for what I could have done myself."

I shake my head. "You keep saying that, but I think it's a load of bull."

Paige stands and makes her way to Jace. "Did you pay him?"

He nods. "That's why I'm complaining. I'm pretty much broke."

"That sucks."

The old man looks over to us, but still doesn't say a word. His dog stands up and starts walking around the room aimlessly.

Paige motions towards the door. "You ready to go?"

I push myself up and follow as they head out.

The dog sniffs my hand as I walk past. I look down at the animal and see gray eyes staring back at me. My hand instinctively makes its way to my gun.

"Don't." The old man sighs. His eyes are the

same shade of gray. "We're here for the same reason you were. No trouble, agreed?"

Beneath his jacket is a black stain that I would have easily missed if he hadn't gotten my attention. I relax a little as the dog retakes its seat next to its master.

"Fine." Androids, whether I want to admit it or not, are just as complex as humans. It seems to be just my luck that I keep running into them. They're unpredictable. I'm not a fan.

The old man looks only to his dog.

I continue onward and close the door behind me. Paige and Jace stand waiting in the distance. Each one says something to me, but I don't catch it. My mind is elsewhere. It amazes me how complex, so many things can really be. Makes you wonder what's hiding beneath the surface.

I don't think I'd have been able to shoot the dog if I'd tried. Canines hold a special place in my heart; always have and always will. It wasn't real, but it was. I don't think I'm making any sense. I'll just be happy when this journey is over.

12
THE DARK IN THE NIGHT

SOMEONE HAS BEEN FOLLOWING us for the last three days. I don't know if Paige or Jace noticed, but I have. It's hard not to. Now I am in no way a paranoid person, but some things should just be expected. If I know Polluck, there's no way he'd just let us go. Not without a tail. Jace has finally calmed down and reverted to his normal self. Saying anything would just bring us back to square one. I'm not the least bit alright with that. In the end it's simple; I'll have to go back and face Polluck again. Maybe not now, but most definitely in the future. There's no doubt that I hurt him this time. Maybe not physically, but definitely his pride. Whoever has been following us has been doing it rather closely. A little too closely for most professionals. They're either super confident or super stupid. I'm sure I'll find out in the next little while.

"We almost there, Wallflower?" Jace keeps moving at the same pace since the clinic. His endurance seems to have gotten far better than when we first started traveling outside of Reno. Either that or he's stopped being a picky eater.

We're making better time than I thought possible.

"Probably." I pause. "Haven't been this way in a while. A fair bit has changed."

Paige yawns and stretches as she walks. "Not really. Still the same old buildings just getting a little bit dirtier."

Jace shrugs. "Dirty is just fine by me. Means it's been well used."

"Or well abused."

He smiles. "I suppose they're the same, aren't they?"

She nods. "Can be. Depends on what your outlook on life is."

Most of their conversations go on like this. I don't know what Paige is playing at but it's almost as if she knows how to feed his ego just enough to make him do exactly what she wants. Is she the reason he's moving faster than he was with me? Maybe. It's hard to tell. I don't know much about Jace to begin with.

"Ever been to St. Joseph's?" Paige glances my way, but I know she's talking to Jace.

He shakes his head. "Where's that?"

"Just past Vancouver. Used to be one of the cities in the sky. Well... Before the war."

I can tell she wants me to chime in and say my two cents, but I don't. We aren't working together just traveling together. Besides, I don't really like where this is going.

"Who name's a city St. Joseph's?" He looks up to the sky. "A city floating on the air needs a better name than that."

"Why?" Paige thrusts both hands in her pockets

as she continues her pace.

"Why? Because it does. It's too religious. I knew people that wouldn't step foot into places just because of their name. A name is the most important part of a place. Give it a name like St. Joseph's and people would expect it to be almost godly."

"That's exactly it. It was too godly. That's why it fell." I don't even realize I've responded until Jace stops walking.

Paige looks at me as if I'd just said something blasphemous. Did I? In my eyes it's simple. Our heads were up in the clouds for a long time, but eventually we had to get thrust back to earth.

"You been there, Wallflower?" Jace reaches into his pocket and pulls out a crumpled pack of cigarettes.

I nod. "A long time ago."

The click of a lighter fills the air. "What's it like?"

"I don't know. It's been a long time."

Paige comes out of her daze and starts a steady walk past us. "It's the same as it's always been."

We make eye contact for just a moment before she turns away. She's been there? Only residents have seen the city. There are no visitors. If Sheila had someone other than me that could have done this job, then I'm sure she would have hired them first. Why do I have the job instead of Paige? She seems more than capable of finishing it herself.

"You been there too? Well now I just feel left out." Jace takes a long drag of his cigarette. "All this running is wearing me out."

I can see it; the subtle changes. I'm caught

between two people I know nothing about and for the first time ever it bothers me. Something distinct shines in the distance. I look past Jace, past the worn-down buildings, to the bridge we went over an hour ago. It's a signal.

"You want to set up camp?" Paige stops and turns back to the two of us. "It's probably about time. We'll be in Vancouver by noon tomorrow."

I'm still fixated on the signal in the distance. "Might not be a bad idea."

Jace tosses his cigarette. "Alright then. Let's see what we have around here."

The shining stops as I pull my bag off my shoulder. I think I'm going to check this out before we decide to go any further.

***

My hand rests on the grip of my pistol the entire walk from our little camp to the signal I received before. Most times weapons are pointless. When you're walking into a disadvantage you rarely have the time to draw before someone drops you with a bullet of their own. Still, just knowing that the weapon is there is enough. False piece of mind. I hate it, but I'd be lying if I said I didn't fall into it from time to time.

"Polluck's worried about you." Isaac. I hear his voice, but that's all.

I take a few more steps before stopping just short of an old bank on the corner of the street. "You mean angry."

"No. He's actually not. If anything, you've got

him scared."

I can't tell where he's hiding. "Bullshit. Polluck doesn't get scared." I turn and look up to all the windows. "Weren't you the one telling me to get away in the first place?"

"True. I didn't even think you should have come back for a lowlife like Jace Marshall. You can't tell me he was worth all the commotion you caused back there. Walking away doesn't mean coming back." His voice echoes, but he can't be too far.

"I made a choice, Isaac."

"I know. Doesn't mean people weren't hurt by it."

I slide the pistol out of its holster. "People always get hurt by something."

"Put the gun away, Teresa. You don't need that here." He whispers, and I swear he's within a foot of me.

I turn swiftly, but there's no one there. My pistol searches for a target that doesn't seem to exist. "What do you want? If you're not going to do anything, but talk then we're done. Go back to Polluck, and stop following me."

A piece of paper drifts down from over my head. It dances randomly until it halts at my feet. I kneel and turn it over. It's an article dated back when eleven fell. "What is this?"

"That is what Polluck wanted you to see. It's a message, nothing more. Finish your job if you must, but I really do think Polluck was justified in his actions. I'm not always on his side, but this time he was right."

My eyes widen as I read the faded words. I stand

and look all around me. "Isaac. Are you sure?" But I get no answer. "Isaac!"

I wait a few moments until I'm confident that I'm standing alone. The paper crumples in my hand and falls to the ground. It's an article alright and in it are several people tied to an organization I can't bear to ever look at. Five people stand in front of the camera. One of them I recognize without a second glance.

How would Polluck have gotten this? How would he have known that this was my job? I'm asking too many questions. I'm getting too involved. Still, if it's true then this changes a lot of things.

According to this, Jace Marshall, the man I've been dragging along across the west coast, is a Paladin. I'm not okay with that. I'm not okay with that at all.

13
THE FRACTURED WINGS

THE KNIGHTS WERE A PART of the reformed opposition party founded sometime after St. Joseph's took to the skies for the first time. Somewhere down the line our paths crossed, and I learned how words have more power than most people care to accept; always have and always will. I was young when I heard Sergio Cross speak for the first time. It was in the middle of a festival; one of many that eleven held for its people. We celebrated as most humans do; with music and dancing. I used to love to dance. It didn't matter where I was or who was around. If I felt like busting a move in the middle a factory assembly line, then I would. Usually made a couple of people smile in the process. That was a bonus. I was such a dork.

"Ladies and gentlemen. I think it's time for a slight change in leadership. Over the years we have forgotten where we came from. We have forgotten the planet we were born on." He stood in a white pressed suit with a metal podium between himself and the crowd of people holding recently won stuffed animals and bags of flavored popcorn.

Behind him was a parade of floats made of all sorts of materials and influences. The museum of human history played on a theme of Greek culture this year. It was my father's favorite by far. He always had an interest in the past. Didn't give the future much thought though.

"This city is beautiful." It sure was. "Look how far we've come. All of us have solved the age-old conflict of expansion. Our fellow man can do anything. Go anywhere."

Looking back, the population crisis was the least of our worries.

"But it's important that we don't forget where we came from. The Earth is still our home first and foremost. No matter what anyone says, flight is only sustained from the ground up."

I'm not entirely sure what part of his speech intrigued me. I don't even know why I stopped walking to listen. There's no explanation, but I feel there should be. Why did we do the things we did? Human nature seems to be the failsafe answer for questions of the sort, but I don't know. That answer doesn't really fit with the scene in my mind. I remember it as an eccentric show. The man was a performer and I was captivated.

"It's amazing. Just look at this, Ter. Strong enough to keep the city up and a whole lot more." My father was a peculiar man. Last, I saw him, everything new and interesting always caught his complete attention. There were sometimes when I could have sworn he was the child instead.

"They're just magnets, Dad."

He shook his head and pointed at the large white

poles floating in the air across from him. "Not just any magnets. Look at them."

I was looking, but I just couldn't see what he wanted me to. "You're such a goof. Come on, we're wasting time here. Lindsay and Sarah already have our seats." My sisters, well, at least the ones I got along with.

"Just remember us during the next election! Remember us and you remember your history." Sergio Cross died when the city plummeted to the ground, but not before saying his piece to the people over and over again.

"Do you think it's the positive or negative force propelling the rides?" He stepped past me and kept his gaze locked on the poles.

I sighed and grabbed his wrist. "Negative, now can we just go?"

"But why?"

"Because we have seats waiting—"

"No. Negative. Why negative?"

The air smelled fresher than it had been in months. The parade was about to start, and I was stuck marveling the wonders of magnetic propulsion when a lone performer jumped from one of the floats. It looked as though he was taking a leap of faith. Wings were strapped to his arms as he made his way up rather than down. For a long moment, I couldn't hear my father's words.

The man soared higher as the float below him set the scene of Icarus taking flight for the first time. The labyrinth was made of metal which twisted and contorted at its base. Daedalus took flight just after he and Icarus spoke to one another. None of us could hear what they said. Might not have even been part of the show.

I don't think this was how it was. I doubt they had aviator goggles in ancient Greece. Creative license I suppose. "I just picked one of the two options."

"Without research?"

I sighed. "Dad, come on. The seats."

He shook his head. "We should have just watched it out here, Ter. I don't have the money to for–"

"We said it was fine." He wouldn't have watched the parade without a seat.

Cross stepped down from the podium and disappeared into the crowd. I wouldn't see him again for a few months.

As my father took his first few steps towards the seating area I looked away from the floats and the performers until several small explosions brought me back. I thought they were fireworks. Perhaps they were a part of the show.

I quickly realized they weren't.

Gunshots.

Ten to be exact.

My father took cover as most people did. I, however, turned my attention back to the floats. Hysteria is contagious. One person screams, and everyone enters a new stage of panic. Icarus fell. His wings were fractured and torn as gravity pulled him from the sky. The landing was harsh.

There were no signs of Daedalus.

The paladins came much later.

***

Vancouver is a city of narrow streets and high buildings. People get lost in the in-between all the time. No matter how many people we pass, the message is clear. This is not a city for the faint of heart. It's expensive, connected, and the center of more trade on the coast than I'm sure most people realize.

I have business here that needs my full attention. Paige knows where I am going. She didn't so much as protest when I left the two of them alone to wander the city. She's still as much an enigma to me as he is. One thing at a time.

"Is she here?"

The woman behind the medium sized desk seems to always be wearing the same gray suit every time I see her. She doesn't look at first. A file of papers rest dissected in front of her. There are no pictures, just words. They must be more important to her right at this second. I'm not overly fond of that.

"Excuse me?"

"You're going to have to wait." She gathers the papers in one swift, but crude motion before finally looking up to me. "Conference call."

I shake my head. "I know that's corporate jargon for 'go away and never come back.' She's in there, right?"

She doesn't answer. Sometimes silence says more than any sentence ever can.

I step around her desk and take about half a dozen strides to the door. By the time she stands I've got one hand pushing open the door to the large office on the other side. The paintings hit me first just like they always do. Standing with her back to me looking out the window is a woman clad in blue jeans and a light green hoody. A steaming mug of tea sits on a cork coaster near the edge of her desk. She hears me enter and turns just enough to glance over her shoulder and put one hand on the grip of the pistol strapped to her leg. I do the same.

For a long time, all we have is silence. The buzzing of the lights fills the room with just enough noise to keep me comfortable. I half expected her assistant to barge in after me, but instead she just closes the door and leaves the two of us as we are now. Too many questions lead to too many reasons to drop something like a bad habit. There's no going back now.

A long few moments pass before either one of us makes a distinct move. Finally, she lets go of her weapon; I soon do the same. Her eyes meet mine as she picks up her mug, crosses the room and takes a seat on the couch to my left.

"Greetings." She takes a sip of tea and puts on a smile much larger than I think I've ever seen her put on before. "What's up, home slice?"

Business. Not pleasure. I've got to keep that in mind.

14
THE QUEEN AND HER TOWER

"Since when do you get all casual?" I take a seat in the chair across from her. "I don't like it."

She smiles and sets her mug aside. "I do it all the time. You're just never there to see it."

"I doubt it."

"Why? Can't I be like the common masses every once in a while?"

"From up here? No."

"You make me sound so..." She pauses. "Unlike myself."

It's hard to tell if I'm right or she is. Sheila and I have a history. One which spans a little shy of mine and Polluck's. We remember things differently; sometimes drastically different and when old skeletons get brought up we always find ourselves in opposite corners of the same ring.

"Remember when we took those crates from Leo and hauled them across the interior?"

I nod. "Of course, I do. Why?"

She sits up and puts both hands in front of her. "I had a dream about it."

"Good for you."

"It was good. Though I kept seeing the old crew pop in from time to time. I had mixed feelings about that. After, of course not during." She reaches into her pocket and pulls out a coin. It's ancient, dated back before the cities fell, but she's always had it on her. "Things just keep changing, don't they?"

The old crew? Hadn't thought about them for a while. "It never stops either."

She picks up her mug and takes another sip from her tea. "So, since we don't seem to be reminiscing on old times, why are you here? Don't you still have a job to do? Paige isn't your convenient tag along babysitter."

There she is: the Sheila I know and remember, minus the suit of course. "Why is she a tag along at all? I don't need her."

She shrugs. "From what she tells me, you do. Polluck was in the way, though I'm not sure why he was in the first place. The route you were on wouldn't have–"

"Your constant spying is bull–"

She raises a hand and looks me directly in the eye. "Language."

Fuck language. "Really?"

"It bothers me, you know that."

I nod. "And you know a lot of things bother me. Doesn't seem to change anything."

Body language speaks more than words. One can always predict what the other person will do based on observing this alone. Sheila, however, sits almost as rigid as a statue. Well, I suppose rigid isn't really the right word. She looks calm and collected most of the time, but when shit hits the fan you just get out of the way. I'm not sure whether this is one such time. The signs are certainly there.

"This job." I watch her carefully. "Some things aren't adding up."

She shrugs. "What does it matter? The money is for the delivery."

"This matters."

"Why? I've given you jobs before. Some that were worse than this and you weren't the least bit inquisitive then."

That's true. This is what happens when I break my own rules. "Who is Jace Marshall?"

There's a long pause drifting between the two of us. Sheila pushes herself out of her seat and starts walking towards her desk. She pulls out the chair, takes a seat and pushes a button on her watch.

The door opens behind us. The woman from before steps in. "Could you get Jonathon to bring up some refreshments?"

She nods. "Of course."

The door closes as Sheila opens the drawer next to her. "I thought you'd be excited to see this job through. It had everything you liked: lots of money, a fair distance to travel, and—"

"A paladin."

She takes out some papers and puts them in front of her. "No, a means to get even."

I turn slightly. "What are you talking about?"

She sighs. "Think of the opportunity. That's all the job is about. Nothing more. Nothing less."

"What opportunity? Isn't this your job?"

"Technically yes, but it's a double contract. I'm just the middle man this time."

I shake my head. "I thought Leo was the middle man."

She laughs. "No, Leo was necessary in finding and getting you to say yes. Just getting you to have a conversation with me is challenging enough. Look, Teresa. I don't really understand why you're here. The job pays a lot so just finish it. You'll probably even have enough to fix that head of yours."

She's right. I would have enough. No more using sloppy technology like a temporary bandage. "It's not about the money. If he is a paladin I'm going to blow his brains out. "

"Language." She holds up a paper. "That would be way too messy." I stand, walk over, and take it from her. "What do you think would happen to a paladin in St. Joseph's? Well, to a knight in general?"

"Probably the same as what I'd do to one out here."

She leans back in her chair. "And that is the opportunity I was just talking about."

The door opens again. This time a short, but fit man comes in with a tray in his hands. "Where would you like this, Sheila?"

On the tray is a plate of chocolate cookies and a pitcher of water. "Just over here."

He makes his way across the room and sets everything down in front of her. "Anything else?"

She nods. "Ah, yes. I should have specified. The cookies with the little bits of candy in them. Teresa doesn't really like chocolate."

"Oh, of course." He hurries out the room and closes the door behind him.

The paper in my hands is a contract request to Sheila from whoever is paying her. I skim the details before looking up. "This tells me almost nothing."

"It tells you what it needs to."

"Is he a paladin though?"

She shrugs. "Yes. Well, he used to be. My sources were unable to discern if he still was."

Either way finishing this job would be taking him to his death. Still, some things still aren't making sense. "And what about Paige? Why didn't you just get her to take him? She already said she's been there."

"Her citizenship was revoked. She didn't just walk out and leave like you did."

Murder crosses my mind. Having your citizenship revoked is usually because of that. I've killed people before, that's not the issue, but it was usually for self-preservation. This is different. Very different. If she killed, then it probably wasn't self-defense.

"Just finish the job and be done with this, Teresa." She stands, picks up a cookie, and starts walking to the door. "Now, if you'll excuse me. Jonathon will be back with your cookie. Feel free to stay and chat for a while." She then takes the gun out of her holster. "I have to have a conversation with someone downstairs. Show yourself out when you're done alright?"

"Right."

She laughs a little. "Cool beans."

The way she carries herself, the way she's always carried herself, never changes. Each step demands respect on its own. I feel sorry for the poor bastard she's going to see.

I don't know what I was hoping on getting out of this. There's a reason I avoid this place, and I'm always reminded of it every time I come back. I never quite feel like I'm the same person when I leave. Too many variables enter and too many scenarios emerge. I suppose this is what I get for asking too many questions.

15
THE CITY THAT FELL

I HAVE NO EVIDENCE. The article was clearly enough for Polluck, but I'm not sure it's enough for me. Who am I kidding? It was enough to drag me further off our route and confront Sheila with a barrage of questions. Not that she answered many of them. My hatred runs deeper than I expected. I'm no better than anyone else.

Downtown has changed. It's brighter than I remembered. All the theaters have their lights on. Must be an exciting bunch of shows on tonight. People are like insects; they congregate to the lights out of some strange necessity. For whatever reason they are fascinating. If they find this city interesting, then I wonder what most people would think about eleven. Towers are the exception though. They are bright no matter what time of day. It's like you have a torch around you twenty-four seven.

"Wallflower, what took you so long? Paige and I were about to go in without you." Jace stands just outside the Vogue with a lit cigarette pinched between his fingers. "If you don't hurry up we're going to miss the show."

My steps carry me forward, but my eyes scream caution. "I hope you don't mean in there." I recognize the venue. "I don't do roulette halls."

"What?" Jace shakes his head. "You're kidding me."

Paige pushes off the wall and hands me a ticket. "I was ensured maximum entertainment from the vendor. These guys are apparently all champs." Her tone seems less than enthusiastic.

I shake my head. "Mindless blood sport. If I wanted to watch two people stare at each other while one of them commits suicide, then I'd have walked about ten blocks that way."

Jace tosses what's left of his cigarette aside. "Come on, Wallflower. Where's your sense of adventure? It doesn't always end in suicide, you know?"

"But it does always end with someone dying. There's nothing adventurous about this. It's crude and I don't like it."

Paige shrugs. "Suit yourself. I'm just along for the ride."

"Wait a minute." Jace sighs. "You mean to tell me that you didn't want to see it either?"

She nods. "Not really, but I am a woman of my word. I said you could pick a show and that I'd watch it with you."

"Well." He stares at his ticket. "That's not right. I don't want to watch something that I can't enjoy with you lovely ladies."

Why am I not surprised? "You can go in if you want. I'll wait out here. I'll know it's an exciting game if I don't hear the shot for at least a half hour."

Jace lowers his head. I don't think he's enjoying my sarcasm. "Way to be a killjoy, Wallflower." He then drops his ticket on the ground and starts walking down Granville Street.

Paige kneels and picks it up. "How are we supposed to get him to St. Joseph's if you piss him off like that?"

"He'll be fine." I hand her my own ticket. "He's stuck with us for this long."

"Just remember you're not the only one with a job to do." A couple of homeless men sit perched upright just to her left. She tosses them the tickets before walking away.

It doesn't matter. I have more on my mind than anyone knows. A man's life could be in my hands. Maybe I'm too full of myself, but what Sheila said made sense. A paladin in St. Joseph's would be nothing short of suicide. Can I walk a man to his death? I don't even know him, really, but if he is what I think he is then it doesn't matter.

That city fell and killed a lot of people. There should be some retribution. There must be. In a world like this sometimes justice is a self-applied concept. I start walking. I think I've just made up my mind.

***

I used to be one of those people in the roulette halls sitting across from someone with an old revolver in between. I was at a real low. They sell it as a means to start again; some crazy baptism. The victor gets a large sum of money. Enough to clear the table and get ready for some new guests. Russian roulette is a game that has been commercialized to the point where everyone at rock bottom realizes they have a choice: die or let fate determine whether you give life one last go.

The smell of death trails off behind us. The road we're on now has one destination and one destination only: St. Joseph's; the fallen city. I am an executioner walking a man to his death. He doesn't know this. I haven't taken the sack off his head.

Paige smiles as she walks, but as we approach I can feel her positivity drop. She has a past here. So, do I. To lose one's citizenship and be exiled means that something unforgivable happened. Perhaps she's walking to her death as well. Where does that leave me then? There's a reason I never went back. Too many faces reminding me of how things were.

"Holy shit. What the fuck is that?" Jace looks up and sees a very bright silhouette in the distance. His reaction is not unique. I've heard many people say the same thing when they've seen St. Joseph's for the first time. Still, his response is strange to me. A paladin would know what the cities looked like.

Paige glances up from her book then goes back to its pages. "That is St. Joseph's. City number eleven."

He pauses. "It looks like a mountain."

I nod. "More like a tall island actually. It's pretty massive."

"How did I not know this was here. Those lights put even Vegas to shame."

I shrug. "It's been here since it fell."

I had forgotten how pretty the city looked in the

evening. From this distance it could be mistaken for a snow-covered mountain if we ever got snow around here that is. My father once described the sight as a miniature in a globe. It's a perfectly preserved image. Not even plummeting thousands of feet could tarnish what the engineers created. Can't say the same for the ground beneath it though.

Despite the beauty there is no one around us. This is ground zero to one of the greatest impacts the planet had ever felt. The earth beneath the city is a graveyard. The people who died were forgotten because they couldn't be found. Humans crushed like ants on a sidewalk. No one wants to be around a place like this.

From this point onward, there is only a flat plane of land between us and the city. We can see everything and everyone approaching which means so can they.

"Is there even a way in? Looks pretty cut off." Jace's walking pace seems to have increased.

"There's a way in."

He smiles. "Are they usually okay with visitors?"

I sigh. "I have no idea."

By the time we cross the distance Jace has smoked three cigarettes, Paige has finished her book and I've started rolling up my left sleeve. The watch lights up. I take it off and stuff it into my pocket.

"What are you doing, Wallflower?"

"Getting ready for the scanner."

In front of us is a very high wall. This isn't like Seattle. This place is on lock down all the time and there is no real way to break in. I continue forward.

Jace goes to follow, but Paige pulls him back. Neither one of them should get closer until the door opens. I'm not entirely certain what will be on the other side. I stop once I reach the wall. A square section no longer than a foot begins to retract. I take a deep breath then place my forearm inside.

Electricity passes in a wave through my circuits. It tingles like if someone splashed warm water on my skin.

"You good, Wallflower?" Jace shouts, but I don't answer.

Nothing about what I'm doing makes me good.

Within a moment the electricity stops. I turn and motion to pull out when the section closes and locks my arm in place. "What the—"

All I feel is something hot being poured on my skin.

I scream.

Jace and Paige move.

The wall begins to open.

I don't know how or why, but the moment two people walk out both Jace and Paige fall to the ground unconscious. They're security. They must be. Both of them certainly look dressed for it.

My arm burns and is still stuck in place. "What are you doing? Get away from them."

But they carry on as if I'm not there.

"Citizen, you are in need of an upgrade." The voice is digitized. Sounds like a machine.

"Like hell I do." The pain comes again. This time in isolated sections. "Fuck!" It's like something sharp is peeling away each layer of skin.

I take a deep breath and try to calm down, but

I can't. My heart rate is too high, and my vision is starting to blur. The clamp is still locked in place. No matter what I do I'm not going anywhere. I close my eyes and start counting to ten in every language I know. I need to stay focused and awake.

The two guards carry Jace and Paige inside.

"Citizen, thank you for your patience. This should only take a few more moments. Please stand by."

Fucking machine. Doesn't look like I have a choice now do I?

I stay there for what seems like an hour. The fluctuating pain has made my arm almost completely numb. The tears have stopped creeping into the corners of my eyes. The clamp finally unlocks, and I fall backwards onto the ground.

"Citizen, your upgrade has been completed. Thank you for your cooperation and have a wonderful day."

I can't stop staring. Beneath the drying blood, precision stitching and metal laced skin is a new set of circuits. These ones are more visible than what was in my arm before.

"Hello, do you need assistance?" Standing at the door opening now is a robot with a big red cross on its chest.

I push myself to stand. "Get out of my way."

It does, and I walk in.

Blood drips down to my fingertips.

16
THE YOUNG DOCTOR

THE SMELL OF ORANGES fills the air. I don't know if it is from some cleaner or an actual fruit basket, but it's the first thing that hits me as I make my way down the corridor. On second thought I doubt it's a chemical. It smells too real.

I walk forward through the vaguely familiar halls; clutching my arm as I go. Several robots have approached me as did the first one. These new circuits must be transmitting to the system or something. I've never been pestered so much in my life.

"Hello, I'm sorry. Where are you going?" That was not a machine's voice.

I stop and turn to the left. "To see whoever is in charge. My companions were taken here while I was... At the gate."

A girl, maybe fourteen or so, stands at an open doorway with her hair up in a net, a mask on her face and her hands covered by gloves. "Then they are probably in security detoxification."

I adjust my stance and start walking towards her. "That is where I need to go."

She takes a step back and looks as if she's about to bolt through the doorway and close herself into the room. "I don't have access to go there."

"Do you know who does?"

"I should take a look at that." Her gaze falls on the bloody mess I'm holding together. "Did you just get your upgrade?"

I shrug. "I wouldn't exactly call this an upgrade."

"It is though. Trust me. It's been out for a couple of years. All of the feedback has been positive."

"Does that include the installation?"

"I couldn't say."

Trust her? I don't even know who she is. Besides, I question her words. I don't think anyone who has had their old circuits ripped out and replaced with such a crude procedure would give anything remotely close to positive feedback.

She steps into the room behind her and I follow because I have no idea where I am going. All the halls look the same. The door closes automatically, leaving the two of us to stare at each other in what looks like a doctor's office. "Your arm."

"Hurts like a mother—"

She turns and picks up a pile of gauze pads. "Don't say that."

"Why not?"

"Because I don't like it. There are better words out there. A whole dictionary in fact. People always seem to favor the crude ones."

I nod. "And why do you think that is?"

She pulls out some containers of clear liquid. "Most people would say that it is because the world is a crude place, but that's not true. People just need to start looking for more of the good. It exists even if you have to search for it sometimes."

"How old are you?"

"Does it matter? I'm old enough." She sits herself down in a chair and motions to the empty seat across from her.

"So, you're a doctor then?"

She shrugs. "I suppose you could call me that."

I take a seat and place my arm on the table. "Well you either are or you aren't."

"Some things aren't black and white, you know?" She gently cleans around the incision.

"No small talk? Fine, but I meant what I said earlier. I need to find the two I came in with."

"Why did you bring them here? They aren't citizens. I'm surprised the doors opened for you in the first place."

"It's my job to take things and people where they need to go."

She pauses. "You're a courier?"

"Yes, that's right."

For a long moment I feel judgment intertwining with the stare she's had on me since I last spoke. Finally, the gauze goes down and the gloves come off. "And an addict too by the looks of it."

"I'm sorry, what?"

She slides her chair back and reaches for a clipboard on the counter. "Your irises are green. Far too green for it to be a normal pigment. Are there microbots in your system?"

This isn't what I signed up for. "It's none of your business."

She sighs. "It is, actually. I'm your quarantine officer and it is my responsibility to make sure you aren't bringing any harmful contaminants into the city."

"Quarantine officer? I suppose you aren't a doctor then." I sigh. "The bots are for my head. I suffered an injury awhile back. They are keeping me alive."

She puts on another pair of gloves. "They are drugs. Probably killing you too. Do you have a dependence on them?"

I consider lying, but there seems to be very little merit in doing such a thing. "Two years between doses. After that the headaches and the withdrawal symptoms kick in."

"They're sloppy machines. Like putting a bandage over a bone fracture. They do nothing in the long run." She grabs a pen and scribbles something onto the clipboard. "And how long have you been away from the city?"

Too long. "I can't remember."

I feel as if I'm in a therapy session of some sort. She's judging me. I know it. Doesn't matter though. This isn't a permanent visit. I just need to get things sorted, get paid, and then go. The hum of the lights overhead isn't helping. It's amazing how silence reveals how annoying things truly are.

Within a few moments the clipboard goes down and the chair slides back over. Her hands are cold. I can feel it through the latex. The mountain of gauze and bandage wrap she applies makes a thick but mobile cast. She pulls off her mask and gloves once she finishes. I suppose there isn't an issue, or she wouldn't have exposed herself.

"Procedure states an overnight stay is mandatory. Especially when someone has spent so much time outside of the city walls."

I pause. Her face; there's something about her. She seems too familiar. She pauses long enough for me to get the hint; she knows I'm staring. "What's your name?"

"Chloe."

That's it, the final piece in check. The door opens behind me to reveal a man at the door. Security.

"This is Carlson. You don't have any contagious pathogens in your system, so he'll be taking you to an observation room. If the results of your stay are what I think they will be then you'll be out in no time."

My eyes don't come off her. "How old are you?"

She shakes her head. "You asked me that before. I'm old enough."

"Chloe, it's me. Teresa. Do you remember?"

She's too young. Maybe it's not her. "Of course, I do."

"Then why didn't—"

"Because all quarantine examinations are to be conducted professionally."

Carlson steps forward. "Ma'am, I need you to come with me."

"Chloe, the people I came in with. Are they safe?"

She sighs. "It's not my area of expertise."

"I'll need your weapons. They aren't allowed once we cross into section three. You can have them back once you depart." My mind isn't even registering his words.

This girl sitting in front me suddenly has my complete attention. There are some things I walked away from which I wish I hadn't, but I wasn't in a good place when I was here last. I don't even think I'm in a good place now. If she was there then I knew everything was going to be alright. Problem was there was no way I could have taken her with me.

"Aunt Teresa."

I look up.

"You have to go."

I can imagine that not many people come through here, but when they do all eyes must be on them. There isn't a move I can make or a conversation that I can have which won't be under surveillance. Welcome home, Teresa. There's a reason I should have stayed away. If there's one person I can't have judging me it's her. Eighteen. She should be at least eighteen. Is my perception of time gone or is it something else?

I stand and walk out the door with Carlson following close behind.

I loved that kid more than I ever loved myself.

17
THE PRICE OF LIVING

THE WAY SHE LOOKED AT ME spelled nothing short of disappointment. That is always worse than someone being outright mad at you. It hurts more and makes you feel shittier. Not a great combination by any stretch. Maybe I deserve her judgment. I don't know what my sister told her; I don't know what she could tell her. I never had the best reputation around here anyway.

"Scanners say you're good to go, ma'am." Carlson's voice echoes through the speaker. Time is up, and I have answers to search for.

The door slides open and there he stands. He's the dedicated type; young but not too young. The way he wears his uniform shows me that he takes pride in this. Whatever this is. "Officer Gev just needs you to sign these forms and then you're cleared to enter the city."

I stand and make my way to the door. "Papers? I thought the process would take longer."

He shrugs. "It's different depending on record and background."

"Oh really?"

He offers a scanner and motions to the open file on the table next to him. "It's not my place to comment on the length of one's stay. Might even have something to do with the holidays. Gev has a soft spot for those coming home to see family."

I look down at the papers. "What is all this?"

"Just the hard copy for you to peruse and take with you if necessary. Present your circuits and I'll scan to receive consent."

I offer my bandaged arm as he takes a small machine out of his pocket. The information passes within a few seconds. It feels like a slight tingle, nothing more. Every few moments the man looks at his watch. I don't know if he's receiving any messages or just wants to leave really bad.

"There were two other people with me at the gate." I pause for a moment. His eyes are fixed on the scanner. "Where is security detoxification?"

He replaces his scanner and turns towards the door. "I'm sorry. I don't have the authority to divulge that information."

"I need to see them."

"You probably won't. Not tonight anyway. Everything is automated until the morning."

"I'm sure we can come to an arrangement."

He shakes his head. "We don't need an arrangement. The answer won't change."

I reach into my pocket. "I have money."

"Not the kind of money we use here." He rolls up his sleeve and shows his circuits. "These are everything now. What we are and what we do are connected with these. You're broke. You have no information and you have no money."

"How do you know that?"

"Your circuits are too fresh." The two of us maintain eye contact for several moments before he smiles and gestures towards the door. "If you want to submit forms for entry then you can do it tomorrow. Until then Merry Christmas. Enjoy the day, ma'am."

Christmas? Is it Christmas? It can't be.

I step outside, Carlson follows. The two of us move down the hallway to what looks like a reception area. There's no one manning the desk.

"Have a good day, ma'am." He breaks off and heads up the staircase to my right.

For a moment everything is quiet.

"Aunt Teresa." Steps echo behind me; quiet ones. Chloe walks up to me with several bags in one hand and a book in the other. "Where are you headed?"

There is something about that question. It sounds more like an obligation than an inquisition. She doesn't look at me, at least not directly. That hurts a little. We used to be so close.

"I don't know." I clear my throat. "I haven't really thought about it."

"What do you mean?"

"I'm here for a job."

She nods. "Oh. I see."

She's staring down at the ground now. The wheels are turning; I can see them. She's contemplating something that she doesn't need to. I have no expectations. I never did. It might even be better if I just kept my distance.

"I'll figure it out." I take a few steps forward.

"Have a good day, Chloe."

"I've been pretty unlucky this year."

I turn. "Sorry?"

"Nothing, just thinking out loud."

She pulls the book close to her chest and moves past me until she's out the door. There's a story here. I can see it in her eyes. Question is, do I want to hear it?

"I hate turkey. Please don't let there be turkey." My steady walk becomes a light jog as I catch up.

The sudden wall of cold air hits me hard. I'm not ready for it. That and the patch of ice now directly under my boot leads to a much more embarrassing re-entrance than I was intending. My balance falters and I end up stumbling several paces past her. "Oh fuck." Wow, that sounded more like a song than a curse.

"Oh jeez. Are you alright?"

I'm shivering. There's snow. Why is there snow? It never snows in these parts.

"Yeah. I'm fine." I laugh a little.

"Okay."

I look up to see the streets painted in a rainbow of lights. It's picturesque; worthy of holiday cards. If they still made them.

Everything is electronic now.

Traditions gradually end up fading over time. It's like some weird circle of life. The lights though, they're timeless. So much more than a mere tradition.

"I'm going to see Mom and Dad." She holds up the bags. "I couldn't make it to dinner last night." She was too busy working and running into me.

"How are they?" I zip my jacket up as high as it will go and thrust both hands into my pockets. Damn, it's cold.

"Temperature regulator has been on the fritz. The council announced it during the last meeting." She pauses. "Sorry, you don't look like you're used to the cold." She takes a deep breath. "But you asked a question. I get side tracked sometimes. They're fine. You could ask them yourself if you want to."

There it is, the question. Well, the question without there actually being a question. "No, it's alright. I need to find a place to stay for the night."

Disappointment, whether she means to express it or not, surrounds her. A small tinge of guilt runs through me, but I ignore it.

It isn't the time.

This isn't some happy story book ending that I can just walk into. I've got to deal with the baggage before I can even step back onto the scene.

"I just want to say..." I'm not sure what I want to say. "Merry Christmas."

So sappy.

So stupid.

I need to go.

"Take care, Chloe." With those words tumbling out of my mouth I start walking, quickly, towards a street I think I recognize.

"Aunt Teresa." She tucks her book under her arm and takes my left hand. A slight tingle races up my arm. "My contact code, in case you need anything."

The look in her eyes is one of pity. I know what she sees, and it hurts more than any physical wound.

To her I am the aunt that left, I am an addict, and a nomad. That isn't what I wanted, at least I don't ever recall wanting it, but maybe it hurts so much because it's true. I am what I am because of what I did to this city and to my family. I helped Sergio, that is my greatest sin. My hands have just as much blood on them as his did.

18
THE DEATH OF A HERO

"THEY'RE COMING, YOU KNOW. You must leave. If you don't they'll get us both." Heavy steps echoed outside. Metal scraped concrete. It was louder than the squeal of Styrofoam being ripped apart in the open air. I remember that room so vividly. The accolades covering the walls were not from one person but an entire team; that is what Sergio had told me and yet when I looked at those pictures, I mean really looked, there was only ever him standing tall with an outstretched hand. Politics are strange. I don't think anything can ever be won as a team as far as they are concerned.

"Teri, I said go. Stop looking at me like a wounded animal." Was that how I was looking at him? I don't know. "I'll be fine."

The carpet was an off white when I first saw it. Sergio always made us remove our shoes before entering. The man was paranoid, but at the time I was too young to recognize it. "No, we need to get some help. I won't leave you like this."

The red was stained deep into the fibers. It was starting to darken and dry as I knelt at his side. I thought he had spilled wine on himself, but then there was the knife. My mind didn't register what it was seeing right away. "Just go, girl. Please."

There was another man in this room as well. He lay face down towards the window overlooking the city. I didn't recognize him. At that moment he didn't matter to me. "Sergio..."

He pushed once; coughed twice. The strength I had seen him have was gone. "The paladins have their missions. We must do our part. We cannot do that if they find us. Go, Teri."

"Who are you so afraid of? Help is coming. The medics, the police, they're all coming."

His eyes widened. "No–"

"And what do you mean by get us? Sergio, that makes no sense." The thing is that it did make sense, but not at the time.

"They won't be helping me when they get here. You still have the disk, right? Take it to Ricky. He needs to get it before–"

A large explosion erupted outside. I was at the window within seconds. I didn't see anything; no fire, no smoke. "What was that?" Several more explosions chained together and echoed in the distance. This time there was smoke. It came up in waves.

Sergio attempted to push himself into a more mobile position. I remember staring out at the sky as it changed from a gentle blue to a very violent gray. The sounds of roaring aircraft carried over the explosions. I didn't know it then, but I was a part of something I hadn't fully understood. The ideals I had invested in were all skewed. I don't know if I had just interpreted them wrong or if I just fell prey to a man's charisma and didn't see what was right in front of me the entire time.

Everything was clear in front of me then though. The situation I had walked into was beyond anything I had experienced before. The city was going to fall, and I didn't know I supported it until it was happening.

"Sergio." I turned and watched him clutch his chest tightly. "Is this us?"

He nodded. "Of course. Now people won't forget where they came from. We're going home, Teresa."

I had the disk.

"This..." There were screams, faint ones, and the smoke just got thicker and thicker with each passing moment. "This is fucked." I turned towards the door and marched out without looking at him. "So fucked."

"Teresa!" He called after me, but I didn't look back. "Take the disk to Ricky. Please! People are going to die if you don't."

But I didn't. I didn't do anything. I stood in the other room staring at the wall like some child about to scream at their parents. The sirens were still coming, but they never made it to us. When the city started its descent, all bets were off. In that moment there was no order, just makeshift anarchy. People did whatever they wanted in the face of fear. I was afraid not for myself, that would have been selfish, but of the false image I helped create.

The impact shook the earth. A lot of people outside of the city died. We, for the most part, walked away with only a few scratches. To this day the biggest shame I feel is not from the words I listened to or the things I helped the knights accomplish; it was from that disk.

I found out later that of all the lies I had listened to him say, Sergio was right about one thing: people were going to die if I didn't act. Because I stayed in that room the disk never made it to Ricky. The files were reboot codes to the backup generators. They didn't want the city to crash; they just wanted it to fall. It would have stopped the descent just before impact.

"Teresa, please!" No matter how many times he yelled, the words were empty to me.

I suppose that is what happens when a person loses all faith in their previous ideals.

***

The skies aren't nearly as gray as they were before. I sit on a metal bench facing the mounds of snow in a small park between streets. Chloe is long gone and that is okay. I should be alone. There's some shit still here that I never really moved on from.

My watch starts beeping in my pocket. I hadn't put it on since the incident at the wall. "Package delivered. Payment will be wired to the usual place. The client thanks you."

Sheila.

I sit up and read the message over and over. Delivered? He isn't in the city yet. He should still be in security detoxification.

"Fancy meeting you here, Wallflower. Please,

don't get up."

"Jace." I turn quickly only to find myself staring down the barrel of a pistol.

He stands tall and clicks off the safety. Neither one of us move. There is no one around. Why would there be? It's a holiday after all. "I just wanted to express my gratitude. You should have your money any time now. The job is over. You can leave." Everything about him is wrong; the clothes, the attitude, even his voice.

"What is going on here?"

He smiles. "Absolutely nothing. There's just some unfinished business I needed to take care of. Your services are no longer needed."

I go to stand, and he pulls the trigger. It happens just as fast as that. There isn't a loud erupting gunshot, but I do feel the tip of something sharp hit my collarbone. My vision goes first, then my hearing, but not before more footsteps crush the snow.

19
THE TUNNEL AND THE LAMP

THERE'S A CHILL IN THE AIR. It's one of those things your body feels before your mind does. I roll onto my back and feel nothing short of a very uncomfortable, solid, floor beneath me. Someone is tapping. Sounds like metal striking metal. I open my eyes to a barely lit room and a roaring headache. I'm essentially sitting in a gaping hole of darkness.

"Creeper." That sounds like Paige. "That is beyond sick. Get away from me."

"And here I thought I was being romantic." Jace, at least that sounds like him.

I struggle to sit myself up. My hands are bound together, and my head won't stop throbbing. Once I'm semi-aware of my surroundings the smell of something rotten hits me hard. It's too dark to tell what it is. There's only a small flickering light across the way. Where the hell am I?

"Touch me and I'll cut your hand off." She's somewhere to my left.

Jace laughs. "I'm not going to touch you, but believe me. If I wanted to I would, and you'd enjoy it. I'd kill you if you didn't."

I try to bring myself to stand, but as I shift forward I quickly realize that whatever is binding my hands is also attached to the wall. Doesn't look like I'm going anywhere for the moment. "Shit."

"Wallflower, is that you?" The light starts moving around.

I try my best to keep still and judge his movements carefully. The rumble of machinery suddenly erupts around us. We can't be outside of the city so, where are we? St. Joseph's doesn't have too many dark hiding places and there is no way he could have smuggled us out.

"Wallflower?" I feel his eyes on me before the warm light hits my face. There's a moment of silence as I gaze into a shadow, an outline, of a person. He kneels and for the first time since I found him he has a genuine look on his face. He genuinely looks like he'll hurt me. "I'm so glad you're awake. I think we have quite a bit to discuss."

"You shot me."

He nods. "Yes, well, I could tell you weren't just going to leave."

"I suppose I should be angry."

He smiles. "Oh? You're not?"

I shake my head. "No, I was going to screw you over. I kind of deserve it."

"Do you hate me, Teresa?" That's the first time he's used my name. "I think you should. I'm everything you hate." His smile widens for no apparent reason. Paige is still struggling in the distance. The sound of clanking metal seems to be getting louder and louder. It doesn't seem to bother Jace though. There's a larger plan here. I was merely the guide. Do I want to know what it is though? My job is finished.

"And what is that exactly? You are just some guy I was going to screw over. Hate never crossed my mind." I'm lying. Sometimes I do that as a part of some dormant defense mechanism.

"But I'm more than that. You know it. I gave you all the clues and lead you down the path to all the answers."

"What are you talking about?"

He sets down the lamp. "This journey was always mine, not yours."

The eye contact is direct. Neither one of us are giving way to the distractions in the room. Paige yells. I don't quite catch what she says. Doesn't matter. The machines roar and the tapping hastens. I doubt we'd be able to fully understand each other if we started yelling while they are going anyway. Jace lifts his hand and touches the chain around my wrists.

"My father used to tell me of this city. I didn't make it in time. Mom and I bought our spots, and everything." He smiles. "And then the damn thing fell and shook the Earth. The knights are legends."

"The knights..." I sit up and look away. "Are nothing but a group of lying bastards."

"You think you're so righteous? No one should be allowed to be above the other. The cities are just another incarnation of social class. The system broke. The only reason people stay away is because they're still afraid."

"And you're going to show them it's alright?"

He shakes his head. "No, I'm going to open the

doors and let the world decide the fate of this city. It's what my father would have wanted."

"And what are you going to do? Blow them open? You'd be nothing but a common Paladin."

"No, I am the original Paladin. The knights were created for me. My name isn't Jace Marshall, he's just someone I made up, it's Jason Cross. My father was a god who brought this city to its knees."

A man will do anything for his family. Sergio once told me that. Are those the eyes of a wronged soul staring at me now or something much worse? I don't know what to say.

"I hate you for being able to do what almost everyone else in this world can't. You have the freedom to come and go as you please."

"It's not all that glamorous, I assure you."

"I think I'd like to see for myself."

"I think you should just kill me if that is what you are planning to do."

I recognized a long time ago that I can be borderline horrible, but nothing compares to the man standing in front of me. Something changes, though. His whole expression shifts the moment I finish talking. The machinery comes to life again. It's as if someone is constantly turning it on and off.

"Why would I want to kill you? There are things you still need to do for me." Jace stands, lamp in hand, and takes a couple steps back. He looks at me for a long moment and then turns to leave.

"So, you're just going leave me here?"

He says nothing.

"Jace?"

Something attracts his attention.

"Asshole."

There are no more words and I have nothing more to say. What kind of man did I just let into this city? He walks away slowly. I don't hear his footsteps, but the light disappears. A few moments pass before my mind shifts into survival mode.

"Paige!" I don't know if Jace is out of earshot and frankly I don't care. The machines finally die down enough for me to try again. "Paige!"

"Holy frick it is you."

I tug at my chains a little. "Tell me you don't have chains around your wrists."

"I don't have chains around my wrists."

"Then can you move?"

"I was being sarcastic."

I shake my head. "Because it's really the time for that."

The machinery goes silent. I can hear Paige struggling. Her chains rattle and ring almost as loud as the machines did a few seconds ago. They don't start up again. There's a sense of calm in the air that had been absent since I woke up. I don't understand all of this. I just don't. When I get out of here I should find a place, order a pizza and sleep on it. I haven't done anything like that in a long time.

Someone turns on the lights.

I'm blinded.

"Hello?" That's a voice I don't recognize. "Hello?"

"We're in here!" Paige yells while I slump back down to the floor and wait for my eyes to adjust.

Footsteps echo. This person walks in a rhythm.

Damn, I really want that pizza.

"You shouldn't be down here."

I can see him now. His back is to me. He's kneeling in front of Paige with some sort of tool in his hand. It looks like we're in a boiler room of some kind. "Hey, that man that was just here, did you see him?"

He turns slightly, eyes only barely glancing over his shoulder. "I didn't see anyone."

The patch emblazoned on his shirt says more to me than anything else in this room. He is an engineer. I sit up straight and think of everything that has been told to me in the last little while. I've really gotten myself into a mess this time. I know where we are, and no one should be here. We're sitting in one of the engine propulsion ducts beneath the city. This machinery once kept eleven in the sky.

He said his name was Jason Cross. I don't know if there's truth to that statement, but I suppose he doesn't have a reason to lie anymore. Whatever he wanted he got. At least for the moment. Yet after all of this I'm still left with disturbing thoughts, the biggest of which won't leave me to think in peace.

Jace knows about this place and never lived in the city.

That is what really concerns me the most.

20
THE PERSISTENT ENGINEER

THE MAN HAS ROUGH HANDS. Every inch looks like it's covered in dust or oil. Something of the sort anyway. Still, with all the filth and grime, one band on his left ring finger is still as clean as ever. It looks like he shines it every so often. A devoted man. Maybe, or perhaps he's just a man who can't let go. It's hard to tell. I've only known him for about five minutes.

"Are you two alright?" He's kneeling in front of me now. Paige stands behind him tracing the lines on her wrists where the cuffs were fastened.

I watch as he holds the same small tool I saw before. It's a knife. "As fine as we'll ever be I suppose."

He presses a little red button on the hilt and I watch as the blade begins to glow a deep yet bright blue. "I'll have these off in a moment."

"You're going to use that?" It's a plasma knife. "I'm not sure I'm comfortable with it being so close to me."

He pauses. "That is how I got hers off. It won't hurt you."

I shake my head. "Those are illegal for a very

specific reason."

He nods. "Yes, but this one is harmless. I adjusted the polarity and have reduced the flow of emissions enough to allow for organic calibration."

Paige stops tracing lines and the two of us make eye contact before speaking together. "What?"

He sighs, cuts the chain, then touches it against his forearm. "It cuts metal not flesh."

Paige steps around him and watches as the chains rattle against the ground. There are still slight vibrations moving through the room. The engineer slips the blade beneath my shackles and cuts through them like they weren't even there. Silence drapes over us for a long few moments until the machines come alive again. Something happens this time though. Rather than the echoes of gears and the whistling of pipes there is a loud crash. The engineer stands and bolts through the door he came in from. Paige and I are left alone for a moment.

"What was that?" She motions towards the door as a second crash bellows through the room.

I'm on my feet now, but I'm not quite sure what to do. Without warning the entire room goes from a slight vibration to a violent shake. "I don't like this. It's like the whole city is moving."

I step out the door with Paige close behind. We take maybe two steps before the shaking gets bad. Paige falls forward and knocks me into what feels like a railing. It's still dark around us.

"Hey, don't move. You might need to hold onto something." The engineer shouts from somewhere across the way. Paige and I do exactly what he says.

Within seconds the shaking starts to die down. I'm then blinded by the sudden flash of lights above our heads. He must have flipped a switch or something. I don't know whether to curse or thank him. My eyes take a moment to adjust for the second time in the last few minutes.

"What the frick is all this?"

I concur.

We're standing in the middle of a giant web of metal walkways and piping of varying sizes. The smell of oil and dirt quickly waft around us. This is a place that hasn't seen people in a long time. Of course, I'm only assuming. I don't know, but the amount of grime left on my hands after only touching the rail would suggest that I'm right. If people were using these walkways, then I feel like it wouldn't have had the chance to build up as thick as it is.

"I apologize. I have to run a fair distance to reset the gauges." His voice comes from above.

I look up and see him leaning over a railing at least twenty feet over us. "How in the world did you get up there?"

"Two ladders and a walkway." He motions behind him. "It's a decent workout."

Paige walks past me towards the first ladder. "Come on. We should find a way out of here."

"Where is here though?"

The engineer grips the sides of one of the ladders and slides down with little effort until he's only a few feet above us. "This is the maintenance shaft to the northeast engine of city number eleven." He sighs. "I've almost figured out the problem."

"What problem?" I pause and climb up after Paige.

He watches as I pull myself up onto the same platform as him. "Why the city won't fly anymore."

"That is because it crashed." Paige looks him right in the eye. "It can't fly. Too much damage."

He shakes his head. "It can. Mechanically nothing is wrong. I've gone over every inch of each engine. I'm just missing something small."

The look in his eye isn't quite determination, but it's close. Now that I can see him clearly, I realize that I am face to face with a man who looks like he's been pushing himself too hard. The smear of grease on his face is several layers thick. He must work at this often if not all the time.

"Why does the city need to fly again? It's been grounded."

"Why shouldn't it?" He leans back against the rail. "I've been working on this since it happened. I can fix this."

"All by yourself?" Paige shakes her head. "That's just stupid."

"I had a team. Lost some in the fall and the others lost their will to work. This is the job I have. It is imperative that I finish it."

Tensions seem to be rising and for whatever reason Paige doesn't look like she wants them to calm down at all. There's some form of passion in her stance. She looks like she's about to break, but I'm not sure why. People do what it is in their nature to do. This man is no different. He has a goal and he may accomplish it, but for whatever reason it looks like it is bothering her.

She steps forward. "It's broken–"

He shakes his head. "In terms of–"

"Leave the pieces alone."

I can see she's getting more and more aggressive. The engineer can sense it too. "Paige."

"No, the city fell, and it should just stay how it is. You get it to fly again and then it'll just fall like last time. People died. A lot of people died. I can't watch that again. Do you understand what I'm saying? I don't care how long you've been working at this. It needs to stop." There are tears gathering in the corners of her eyes.

I watch as the engineer stands there and judges her words. He doesn't say anything right away. I'm not sure he needs to.

He touches the ring around his finger, takes a shallow breath, and then bows slightly. "I'm sorry you feel that way."

I've never seen her act like this before.

"Thank you, for freeing us. We've had a rough encounter and I don't want you to think that we aren't grateful." I slowly move between them. "We should go. How do we get out of here?" I can feel Paige's harsh stare, but I ignore it.

"Just follow this walkway. After a while there will be a door then an elevator. It'll take you to the power station in the middle of the city." He doesn't take his eyes off Paige. "I didn't mean to offend you."

In that moment she walks and doesn't look back. I thank him one last time before following her. Once we're a fair distance away I grab her shoulder and turn her to face me. Her eyes are red. Looks like she's about to break.

"What is wrong with you?"

She shakes her head. "What that man is doing is stupid."

I sigh. "Trying to repair the damage from before? It's not stupid. He's fixing some people's mistakes."

"If it went back up then it would fall again, and I won't watch more people die. I refuse."

In this moment I am reminded that everyone has their silent demons. I know no more about Paige than she knows about me and, yet I can understand what she means. The future isn't certain. Who knows if that one man can even do what he is trying to. Some believe that St. Joseph's fell because of the arrogance that spewed from its exhaust vents to the ground below. That might be it, but I'm more inclined to believe something slightly different. It fell for the same reasons wars always start: you can't please everyone. And the ugly truth is that there are people who believe that if not everyone can be pleased then no one should be. Humans are such a pain in the ass.

21

THE INTRINSIC ASTRONAUT

THERE'S A BITTER AFTERTASTE in the air. It hits me the moment the elevator doors slide open and we come up to street level. The sight in front of me is a stark, almost extreme, contrast to the snow falling when I came out into the street before. It's warm, almost warm enough to discard a layer of clothing.

Paige steps past me the first moment she gets. I'm not one to pry, but there is clearly something here that is making her act like she is now. I don't know her very well, but this whole mode seems wrong. She's not focused, nor does it look like she'll calm down. Still, regardless of what is happening she needs to bring back some composure. She's still standing in a city which she can't really be walking freely in. I remember Sheila mentioning that her citizenship was revoked.

"Paige."

She keeps walking. "What?"

I jog to her side. "We need to regroup." She turns, but I catch her arm. "Now. Before security comes by."

"I'm not afraid of them. This is my city too. They

have no right to throw me out the door."

"They have every right. How did you get out of detoxification?"

She pauses briefly before pulling her arm away. "Doesn't matter."

"That's bullshit."

"You need to drop it."

I shake my head. "No, I need to know if we should be taking a more discreet route to wherever it is we're going. You're not a citizen, remember?"

"I am a citizen." She turns away and storms towards the street. "I will always be a citizen."

The look in her eye is one that I've seen many times before. I used to have it myself when I was young and quite a bit stupider. I have no idea where to go from here. Home is out of the question. Especially when Jace is out there somewhere. He was so different. Definitely not the same person I went up the coast with.

"I'm sorry." I don't know where the apology comes from. I just say it. The situation seemed to warrant it.

In that moment she pauses and turns slightly. She doesn't look at me. Her eyes are fixed off into space. She's zoning out. "We should go to Helen's."

"What's that?"

Now she looks up. "Are you kidding me? How have you lived in this city and not been to Helen's?"

"You say that like it's blasphemy."

"That's because it is." She pauses before regaining her posture. The subject of conversation is about to change, I can tell. There's a certain look people get when they're preparing to say something that drastically changes the tone. "Look, I didn't mean to be short. I just don't like talking about how I left the city. It was ludicrous." She sounds sincere.

"It's fine. I'm over it."

"Of course, you are."

The sudden emergence of people startles both of us. It's like the doors to every building have opened at the same time. The circuits in my arm start to pulsate. The streets are filling quickly. I don't miss this. Everyone's day has officially begun. I never liked living on a generated schedule.

"This way. We should take The High to North Point." Paige motions to the left.

I shake my head. "You're funny. That's practically the main walkway. Scanners are everywhere that way."

She shakes her head. "Not anymore."

"How do you know that?"

She shrugs. "I still have a few friends around here."

I can feel some of the stares begin to focus on us. We aren't from around here anymore and it is quite evident. Everywhere we step leaves a blemish on the street. It's because we just came from outside and there's a little more than dirt on us. Our clothes are dull and faded compared to the wave of colour that flows around us. We stick out and that isn't exactly a good thing.

Paige starts walking and I follow without hesitation. A few blocks later and we hear sirens. There's a hell of a lot of running and a little bit of climbing, but we make our way unscathed. I'm not going to be doing this every time we turn the corner. We need to find some way to blend in.

***

The longer we walk the more I realize just how much the city has changed. It's livelier than I remember it being. Across the way a group of kids huddle around a small pit with metal marbles in their hands. I didn't know anyone still played with those. The slight hum of a violin traverses between the tall buildings. It's calming; almost mystical. Paige pauses for a moment and takes a deep breath. A slight smile appears, but I'm not sure why. Her next steps are confident ones. In front of us stands a restaurant next to the lobby of a rather grand looking hotel.

"You sure you've never been here?" She glances over her shoulder and thrusts her hand into her pocket. "Best place to eat. Menu changes every month so there's always something different here."

I shake my head. "No, but it looks a little too rich for me. We don't really have any money, you know. If you're hungry–"

"Except for the turkey sandwiches. Those are always there." A beautiful, albeit long, holograph rests emblazoned on static paper in the front window. A letter? The writing is elegant. "These are Helen's rules. They're not difficult to follow."

"You call these rules? What language is that?"

"French. Basically, it says that only BFFLs can enter anytime they please."

I pause. "I don't get it."

Paige opens the door and steps inside. "That's because you don't know Helen."

"What does that even mean though–" The moment I go in I find myself face to face with a giant stone cat. It looks angry. Not sure I understand why it's so close to the entrance. Leaves a fair first impression though.

The place is beyond full. I hadn't noticed right away because everyone sits rather quietly at their tables. No one looks up from their plates. The smell of turkey hits me hard. I've just now become aware that I am hungry. Paige walks past the host into the dining room. He looks up and takes several steps around the podium.

"Ma'am, please... Wait a minute. Paige?"

She nods. "Cameo."

He smiles and goes straight for the hug. "You took your sweet time coming back."

Her return hug is beyond awkward. "Only a few years." She steps back and looks into the room.

"Really? I could have sworn it's only been a week."

She nods. "The enhancements are messing with your perception of time again."

"Sorry, it's rather inconvenient."

"Where's Helen?"

More than a few people have looked up from their tables now.

He shrugs and motions towards a small hallway. "Ask Reba. I haven't seen her all day."

"Thanks."

He pauses long enough to look past Paige directly

to me. "And who is this? A fellow commander?"

She shakes her head. "No. Not even good enough to be considered a candidate."

Commander?

Before I can speak she's already started walking. The host stares at me and starts laughing. "Yeah, she does that sometimes."

I hurry after her but stop when I see her leaning against the wall chuckling to herself.

"What took you so long? You know I've been waiting forever." A short woman stands on a stool facing into the kitchen pass. Two plates of food sit in front of her.

"Reba."

The woman turns. "Ah, Paige. You're back." She steps off her stool and walks away from the pass. Her tone didn't change. I can't tell if she's angry or just annoyed.

I sigh. "Isn't she going to get those to the dining room first?"

Paige shrugs. "When she feels like it."

"It's good to see you." No, not annoyed. She just seems to only speak in one tone.

"It's been a week and you didn't call in." She sighs. "These shifts are killing me."

I look at Paige. "Why do they both think it's been just a week?"

"Who's this?" Reba looks straight at me.

"A courier." Paige pulls a small card out of her pocket. "I'll tell you about it later. Where's Helen?"

"In the back making posters."

"Thanks."

Paige moves, and I follow, but not before Reba

steps in front of me slightly. "I'll be watching you."

I don't respond.

That was weird.

I'm not sure where we're going, but the hall we go down progressively gets more colourful as we continue forward. The arch at the end has no door. The wall past it looks like a giant whiteboard with hundreds of notes made with different coloured pens. Sitting hunched over a clipboard is an averaged sized woman with slight blond hair. She hears us coming and sits back as we walk in. I assume this is Helen.

"What are you doing here? Didn't you call in saying you weren't coming back?" Finally, someone seems to have a decent grip on time.

Paige throws the card on the table. "I need my circuits back."

"Ooh... Commy, that's not going to happen."

I step to the side. "Commy? Who's Commy?"

Helen turns her attention straight to me. "Paige. Who else would I be talking to? You?"

"Maybe."

"Yeah... No." She shakes her head. "You're not a Commander. I can tell. Don't have the training."

"What is that?"

Helen turns to Paige. "Where did you meet her?"

She shrugs. "Why you want to give her a job?"

"Fuck no."

I suddenly feel very out of place in this conversation.

"Your circuits are dead. That was part of the deal."

Paige takes a seat in the chair to her left. "HB, please. It's important."

A long silence drifts between them. I find myself standing off to the side picking at the bandage on my arm.

"The mission is over. You took one for the team, remember? I go back on that then Cameo and Reba have to go too."

Paige clenches a fist.

Helen takes a sip from her water bottle.

"What are you two talking about?" I push off the wall. "Paige where did you take me?"

There's a slight pause before Helen starts laughing. "Just a restaurant."

"This is a restaurant?"

"Yeah. Didn't you see the people?"

Paige nods. "I took you to a restaurant, because I needed to talk to my operations contact. I'm an aerospace explorer."

"Were." Helen takes another drink. "Program's dead."

"Oh, I'm sorry. I didn't know you had company." The voice comes from the door.

I turn and see Chloe standing at the arch with some files tucked under her arm. We make eye contact for a moment and then she breaks it equally as fast. Neither Paige nor Helen say anything, but I'm sure they can sense the tension. You'd have to be stupid not to see it. Neither one of us speak for the longest time.

Someone shatters a plate outside.

For a moment I forget where I am.

This place is too strange to be a restaurant.

22
THE TRUTH ABOUT FAMILY

THE ROOM IS DARK. Only the computer screen illuminates the void around me. Outside, Helen and Paige continue the conversation that started when we got here yesterday. The shouting has increased though, but I'm not sure who it is being directed at. This is how it's been since then. We're laying low like a couple of criminals when there's a man out there who could be doing anything. I need to find Jace, but I also feel the need to understand Paige as well. I don't know why, but I feel like I'm staring at a puzzle and all I can do is try my best to determine the shape of the pieces.

Then there is the engineer. Jace brought us to a place he couldn't have known existed only to find this man. I feel very much like I've been guided obliviously along a journey like a dog following a master I didn't realize I had. That bothers me the most. I am in control not some nobody I picked up off the street.

"Commander is a rank awarded to an individual who has successfully graduated all training programs required to pilot a prototype shuttle craft. These initiates are in the top three percent of their class and demonstrate extraordinary talent in their chosen area. Biometric enhancements are then installed within the nervous system network to augment the body and to subsequently help the Commander complete any and all objectives with ease." Listening to the computer-generated voice is worse than trying to stay interested in a boring person.

The door opens.

A flood of light spills into the room.

"Aunt Teresa." Chloe stands at the door with a glass of something in each hand. "Didn't you listen to that yesterday?"

I did, but I still don't understand it. "I just don't get it."

She sets a glass down in front of me. It's water. "The information is right in front of you though. St. Joseph's is a city of innovation and constant research. It's not like Voltza or Hereford."

I haven't heard someone talk about the other cities in a long time. "No, I suppose it isn't." Maybe that is why I never really fit in here. Science was never a passion of mine.

"If you want to know more, then just ask Paige."

"She's the kind of person who keeps things to herself. I don't blame her, and it isn't my place to pry."

She nods. "But you're curious."

"Of course."

Chloe takes a seat next to me. "Paige's chosen area was Survivalism, you know?" She smiles.

"Reba's was Psychology, Cameo's was Relations..." She pauses. "...and mine was Medicine."

My eyes widen. Awkward silence slips between us for a few moments. "Chloe–"

"We were going to be famous. The first explorers in space since before the cities, but the aftermath and the damage of the fall took too many resources away from the program. It was shut down a few years later."

"That's bullshit. You were only a child. You can't tell me that you were doing this."

She takes a sip of water. "Mom doesn't know I'm here. She'd worry too much if she found out." She sighs. "I'm very smart. That's how I finished school so quickly. I fit perfectly into everything this city stands for. People here will do anything for the sake of science. The city council was always at my parent's door in one form or another."

"The timing doesn't make sense."

She nods. "Of course, it doesn't. I'm just like them. The enhancements affect everyone differently. Reba and Cameo have lost their perception of time altogether. Our bodies don't age nearly as fast as they should. Same with Paige."

"What is the point of that? Why would anyone enhance people?"

"So that we would survive." She takes another drink. "Space is hazardous. Aging is the least of the side effects though."

I'm sitting here listening to a girl who I thought I watched grow up with a carefree life. Did I miss something? Were the signs there? She used to dance spontaneously and pretend to be a ninja in the middle of the living room for everyone to see. "Your mom doesn't know?"

"No."

"What about your Dad?"

She sighs. "He found out, but only much later."

There are so many things wrong with what she has just told me, but I don't know if I have a rite to truly comment on it. She isn't my child, but somehow it feels as if that doesn't matter. I remember why I left this place. It's because I didn't need bullshit like this. The city falling was just the breaking point.

"Why are you sitting in the dark anyway?"

A change of subject? "You can't expect me to believe that this place is some kind of refuge for an abandoned program." I ignore her question completely. "Expeditions to space were never on any political platform. This is impossible."

"Why?" She leans back in her seat. "Just because it wasn't advertised doesn't mean it never existed. Look at Paige, she's practically a walking machine. The amount of chemicals in her bloodstream and bio enhancements beneath her skin weren't put there so she could live in this city."

"What?"

"She's strong and she's fast. Don't tell me you didn't notice."

I take the glass of water in front of me and quickly down its contents.

I did notice.

A door slams in the distance. The shouting has finally stopped. Question is who was the one who just left. Both Chloe and I step out and see Paige standing tall with her back against the wall. She doesn't move as we enter. A light knock follows through the recently slammed door.

"Is everything alright in there?" Sounds like Cameo.

Paige pushes off the wall. "Yeah, Helen is just pissed."

I don't think I've seen her anything other than pissed.

Chloe moves past me towards Paige. The two of them make brief eye contact before the door opens. Cameo steps in, holds it open for Reba, then closes it behind him. It's quiet though their body language says more than words ever could. It's as if they're communicating silently between each other. I'm an outsider watching in.

Without prompt Cameo wraps his arms around Paige as the tears start rolling down her cheeks. It's like he knew she was going to break down before even she did.

I don't know what happened to her or why she can't be in this city, but she has a family here and they've missed her. Only an idiot wouldn't be able to see it. There's respect among those four. I can't help but be a little bit envious of that.

23
THE DECLARATION OF WAR

THE CHATTER IS CONTAGIOUS. I don't think I've conversed for this long on such a large range of subjects since before this began. It's strange actually; I rather enjoy listening to nonsensical things. Cameo is quite the wordsmith. You wouldn't be able to tell at first by looking at him, but it's true. He sits the closest to me on this tiny leather couch. Reba is the farthest, playing with her circuits and Chloe stands with Paige off to the side. I'm a fifth wheel, and yet I still feel a little included in what is going on.

"Teresa, I think we need to talk about what we're going to do from here on out." One simple sentence and the room erupts into silence. Paige shifts slightly. "As much as I want to, we can't stay here for too much longer." She said we. I suppose that means she plans on us sticking together a little while longer then.

Chloe nods. "We'll have to shift our resources around. Audits are coming up."

"What does that mean?" I turn. "There are audits?"

Paige leans against the wall. "Just to make sure

the program stays dead. I don't want to put Helen in a bad spot."

Clearly whatever happened isn't a forgivable offense. "Alright. What did you have in mind?"

"Something a little unconventional."

Cameo is staring between the two of us, but Reba hasn't so much as looked up from whatever it is she's doing. What other place would offer refuge in the city? Sooner or later they'll find Paige and eject her without so much as a second thought. It's bad enough that they let me in without much of a fuss, but I suspect Chloe had something to do with that.

"Where would Jace go? I think that is the real question." I've put off searching for him for long enough.

"Every main street in the city has at least one scanner on them." Reba shifts in her seat and continues fiddling with her circuits. "If there's someone else without circuits then he'll be found."

I smile. "They haven't found Paige."

She sighs. "What makes you so sure they haven't?"

Cameo shrugs. "Realistically, they probably have. It's just that no one wants to go toe to toe with Helen. Piss her off and the city goes sideways."

I look to Chloe who simply nods in agreement. "The number of things she manages for the council is a little scary sometimes."

Without warning my circuits begin to glow through the bandage. Reba's, Cameo's and Chloe's all do the same. Paige looks around for a moment before moving closer. I gently unravel the fabric binding until the glow all but blinds me. I had forgotten about these messages. The council only sends them out occasionally.

"Citizen, please be advised of a mandatory census. All residents must report to the atrium in two days' time for download. Failure to do so will result in loss of circuit functionality." The voice is almost identical to the one at the gate from before we entered the city.

"They say mandatory like they can make you." Paige stands with her arms crossed now. The tone in her voice is like what it was when she was talking to the engineer.

"And it's that attitude that got you reprimanded in the first place." Helen stands at the door with an over-sized water bottle in her hand. "If they say mandatory it means mandatory."

"A census though? I wonder what they're announcing." Cameo pulls down his sleeve and sits back as far as he can into the couch. "Better be worth the trip."

"The atrium isn't that far away." Reba sighs. "There's probably going to be an election. We do have a vacant council seat."

Chloe shakes her head. "They won't fill it. It's a seat for the people's voice remember?"

A symbolic courtesy. That's what that is. The glow from my circuits finally dies down and I'm left staring at healing scars. I did this to myself I suppose. The chatter recommences, but this time it's different; now the subjects are of politics and principles. Paige and I make eye contact for a long moment. She motions towards the door and I follow without hesitation. Chloe is the only one who seems to notice our departure.

"What are your feelings on the underground?" She shoves both hands into her pockets.

I shrug. "Not overly positive. It's not my scene."

"I'm almost certain that is where he is?"

"Jace?"

She nods. "Who else?"

"That is one of the richest areas in the city."

"And the one with the least number of scanners. Once you get verified it's pretty much a free for all. Art and expression with limited technology." She's right. I hadn't even considered the underground as an option. Might even be the best place for her as well.

"What are you suggesting?"

"Just that we can't stay here."

"Is he really that dangerous?" Chloe steps towards us. "The man you're looking for."

I suppose I don't really know. "He just hasn't been up front with us."

Though neither was I.

I'm such a hypocrite.

"We should go now." Paige looks back at the room for a moment. "Before the goodbyes get long and sappy."

I know what she's doing. I've done it before. No one likes a long goodbye especially if you don't know if you're coming back. Chloe watches as we turn away and a wave of instant déjà vu hits me hard. Paige starts walking but I don't. Not right away.

"I'll tell Mom you said hi." She's beside me

now.

The door opens and Paige steps outside. At first, it's quiet, but then I hear a click; a very distinct click. I don't even realize what's happened until Paige falls back into me and I in turn end up on my ass back inside the entrance of the restaurant. How she's still standing is beyond me. Blood seeps from the new crater in her chest.

Someone yells, I think it's Chloe, and Helen is out in front of us faster than I think I've seen anyone move. The woman is fearless. The look in her eye is one of pure fury. Reba and Cameo pull Paige back inside, and it looks like it takes all their strength to do so. She stands grounded like a statue. There are words called out, but I don't hear them. Paige collapses only after Helen steps out and shuts the door behind her.

More clicks sound off in rapid succession.

There's blood on my face but it isn't my own.

Paige looks at me for a moment before closing her eyes.

24
THE PATH TO ANARCHY

I'M IN THE MIDDLE OF A SCRAMBLE like a child witnessing a playground brawl. In a matter of minutes, the tone of the day has shifted drastically. The room has gone dangerously silent. Chloe is bent over Paige with a first aid kit ripped open next to her. The contents are all over the floor. Cameo is there as well, assisting where he can, and Reba is at the door cautiously peering out through the window.

"What the heck?" Paige sits up abruptly and pushes both Cameo and Chloe off her. "That wasn't fair." She clutches her chest tightly. "Shooting me when I'm not ready."

"Lie down. You're tough, but not that tough." Cameo forces her down with as much strength as he can muster.

Chloe tears open a large pack of gauze. "Pressure. The bleeding hasn't quite stopped."

Reba glances over and shakes her head. "What a mess. Getting those stains out of the carpet is going to take forever. You couldn't have fallen outside the restaurant?"

Paige shakes her head. "Thanks, Reba. Love you

too."

I stand slowly and try to take in the scene. Nothing makes sense. "How are you—"

The front door slams open. Reba jumps out of the way as Helen re-enters with her fists clenched. Her knuckles are torn, and splotches of drying red darken the ends of her sleeves. "You two aren't going anywhere. Not until I make a phone call." She disappears around the corner just as fast as she arrived before.

"Frick." Paige sits up again and removes the gauze from her chest. The bleeding seems to have stopped, but the wound is still very open.

I can't look at it.

"Don't get up. I still need to close the wound." Chloe pulls her back. This all seems normal to her.

Cameo shakes his head. "I'd just leave her, Chloe. Give her a couple of hours and she'll be fine anyway."

"She's going to make it worse though."

Paige sighs. "I'm standing right here."

Reba walks beside me and grabs my arm. "If you're going to be sick do it over here."

I pause. "No, that's not it. What the fuck was that?"

She shrugs. "Paige is a survivalist. She has the parts installed to prove it. It takes more than one well-placed bullet to take her out. Good thing too."

"Why?"

"Because if she kicked the bucket Helen would have torn apart half the city to find who was responsible. It may not seem like it, but she cares a lot. Paige is part of the family. Always will be." Reba lets go and starts a slow walk towards the bar. "I don't know about you, but I need a drink."

Finally, something that makes perfect sense in this place.

***

"Stop looking at me like that." Paige sits across from me with a hand on her lap and a plate of untouched food in front of her.

"Like what?" I don't sound convincing. Not in the slightest.

She shifts carefully before choosing her words. "Like I'm a freak."

Of all the words I would have chosen, freak would not have been one of them. That word would make anyone sound like nothing short of a monster. I am a lot of things, but a monster isn't one of them. Her words sting like a slap in the face. I don't think she's a freak, but I can understand why she feels that way. I'm the outsider; I'm the one without the context. This stuff is beyond me. I don't think I want to try and understand it.

"Paige." For a second or two that's all I can manage to say. "That's not—"

"It's ok." She sighs and picks up her fork. "Being a self-aware Zombie when I get hurt is part of what I signed on for." The wound in her chest is still very open. "I'm not indestructible. We should probably be more careful."

"Yes, you should." Helen steps in with Chloe following closely behind her. "That generator of yours is for minor injuries nothing more. Too much strain on it will kill you just as fast as that bullet would have."

Generator?

Cameo and Reba walk in through the door to my left and take a seat in the two vacant settings of the table. "Well, that certainly was eventful."

Reba shakes her head. "Not the time, Cameo."

"Not even close." Helen shakes her head. "Smart people. They waited just until you were outside."

Paige laughs. "Literally just outside."

"Regardless, I think it's very well established that it isn't safe out there. We need to get you out of the city." Helen's gaze rests on Paige and Paige alone. "But not until this has blown over. I'll put pressure in the right places until then."

This doesn't sit well with Paige. I can tell by how her posture shifts.

"We should probably worry more about the census the council has just called." Chloe steps close to Reba. "And the person you two are looking for."

Jace. His name, or at least the one he told me, has been one of the only things on my mind since we got here. This city enrages me. I want to leave, but too many things are keeping me here. I don't like that. I don't like it at all. It's as if the freedom I had worked towards is all but gone. I'm sitting at square one when I passed it a long time ago.

"There have been some reports coming down the grape vine." Helen pulls up a chair and sets her water bottle on the table. "Apparently there's a gathering of sorts approaching the walls."

Cameo sits forward. "What kind of gathering?"

Helen shrugs. "Fuck if I know, but whatever it

is has quite a few people spooked and then there's a census being called. I doubt it's a coincidence."

St. Joseph's is a city of legend to most people outside of its walls. The fact that there are citizens with genuine fear for what is outside of it is worrisome. Now, there have always been people who were scared, but this is different. I can tell by how Helen says it. She's unsure, but her confidence doesn't waver in the slightest.

"What's the play then, HB?" Chloe asks the question to Helen, but looks between all of us for some sort of reaction.

"We need to know more before anything else happens. Cameo and Reba will go to the underground. Maybe they'll find out more about your mystery man." Helen looks directly at me as she says this. "Paige is going to stay here for obvious reasons. The rest of us will go to the census as instructed. Maybe we'll be able to learn more about this Polluck while we're there. Something will be announced, I'm sure."

My expression changes. There isn't a single person in the room who doesn't notice. "Polluck? What does he have to do with this?"

Helen takes another sip of her drink. "It's the name that came up in connection with the gathering. Our information on the situation outside of the walls is very limited."

"Well, that's convenient. Teresa and I have met him before. The council has a rite to be worried."

I can feel Paige's stare on me. "He's a dangerous man."

My words are empty. I'm lost in thought as I say

them. Jameson doesn't back down. He shouldn't have come here. Why did he come here? The question is redundant and unnecessary. I know why he's here. Paige doesn't break her stare. The moment we make eye contact is like an electric circuit being completed. The recognition is mutual. Could he break into this city? Doubtful, but he would try. I know he would. That is scarier than the thought of him making it inside.

25
THE INTANGIBLE PHANTOM

WHAT WE DO TO OURSELVES defines who we are not only as people, but as a society as well. Most wounds we receive, whether intentional or not, are self-inflicted. I've come to this realization before. There is a man on the balcony overlooking the atrium. His gaze is one of knowing. The men beside him show no hint of this. I spot him instantly. The man just stands out. He is an outsider amongst his peers. Wouldn't surprise me if he despised this city as much as the outside world.

"Citizen, once the download has been completed, please wait for word from the council." The same message has been echoing every few minutes like clockwork. It irritates me, but I look to be in the minority. Everyone around acts as if this is some honor or privilege.

It's not.

The look on the man's face confirms it.

"If you stare long enough maybe he'll notice you." Cameo stands next to me with a small notebook in his hand. "I don't think you want him to though."

I turn, but just enough so that I can still see the

man. "And why not?"

Cameo smiles. "That's Helen's man."

The download itself was quick and painless. Reba took the longest, but that is only because she had a dozen questions to ask before presenting her arm. She's feisty when she wants to be.

"This is a waste of time, you know?" I look up at the buildings and see more of the same grey, lifeless, hue. "Rather than having people download upgrades—"

"For someone who used to live in this city you sure do a lot of complaining." Helen takes a sip from her water bottle then looks over to me. "Is the world out there so much better than in here? If it were then I think we'd have more citizens walking."

"There are enough of us out there."

"I don't think so." A crowd starts forming around the center of the atrium. "No one leaves because this city is good to us. Even Paige is trying to fight her way back in."

I nod. "The city isn't good to everyone."

She nods. "Because not everyone can be pleased."

"Citizens, please give your full attention to the council." The message has changed.

A line of men stands on the balcony looking down on us with different expressions. The most prominent; however, is the man in the middle. He's the only one leaning forward enough to see the people directly below him. "Citizens." His voice is clear and commanding. "The download you have all received requires an upload in a week's time. This is simply to update our records. There is no mandatory gathering as the information will flow automatically without prompt."

Reba shakes her head. "We could have done that without gathering, genius."

He pushes off the balcony. "However, this is not the reason we asked citizens to gather today. The census is, how shall we say it, housekeeping for municipal records. There is a matter which the council needs to discuss with its citizens. There is a gathering of sorts cultivating outside of our walls. Counsellor Ferdinand has more of the details."

The man I noticed before steps forward and looks to the crowd as the other man had. "Surveillance has shown an increase in motion to the south. We believe this to be the first steps of a hostile engagement." Some people begin shifting nervously. "We have gathered here to vote on the action to take."

Another counselor steps forward to speak. "We as a council have already cast our votes, but we find ourselves at an impasse. The people's vote is necessary to move forward in any course of action."

The first man moves beside Ferdinand. "It has come to our attention that the man outside of our walls is highly dangerous. His intentions are unpredictable, but highly probable to be violent in nature."

The counselor on the end leans against the balcony. "We can either go to him, hold a civilized conversation, and negotiate if need be."

"Or." Someone breaks the line of counselors and moves to the other side of Ferdinand. "We can trust our information and bring the fight to him. This man's presence is not to be taken lightly."

I turn to Cameo. "That's him."

"Who?"

I look back. "Jace. The one Paige and I are looking for."

"All citizens have twenty-four hours to cast their votes. The result will be announced at this time tomorrow. Please note that violence is not the intent of this council, but the protection of its citizens is our top priority."

And with those parting words the men step back away from the balcony and return through the doors they emerged from. Jace pauses, and looks out one last time. It's hard to tell from this distance, but I swear he's smiling as he turns and heads back inside.

"How is that even allowed?" I turn to Helen. "That is him."

She nods. "I have no fucking clue."

The whispers have already started to drift around us. There isn't a single person here who is silent. The words are different, but the subject matter is all the same; talk or fight. I've heard all the conversations before. I've walked in the middle of them. Running packages between neutral roads teaches you about the effects of violence.

I don't know this city well enough; not like I used to. The vote can really go either way. That just means I'll have to act before the people have made their decision.

***

"I know that man." Chloe pulls out a chair and sits herself down. "I've seen him talking to Carlson."

Carlson? "I'm sorry who is that?"

She sighs. "I work with him. He's a guard. I'm pretty sure he was there when you were in quarantine."

"Him?" I pause for a moment and gather my thoughts. "Do you know where he is? We need to have a conversation."

"Yes, but..." She shakes her head. "I don't think that would be a good idea."

"Chloe, I need to find some answers. This whole thing is driving me insane."

Reba pulls out a chair and takes a seat between us. "So, what are we talking about?"

I shrug, but Chloe responds. "I think Carlson knows that guy Teresa is looking for."

She nods slowly. "Oh, I see. That is a bit of a problem."

"Why?"

Reba turns her attention to me. "Because there was a thing." She then turns to Chloe. "I'll leave you to explain that."

Chloe shoots her a look of pure disgust. "Do I have to?"

Reba shrugs. "You don't have to do anything, but she looks pretty curious."

She glances at me before letting out a low sigh. "We went out for a while. Things didn't work. I don't really want to go there."

"I see." I can tell the subject is a little

uncomfortable for her. "You could just tell me where he is, and I can go myself."

Reba cuts in before she can say anything. "It's fine, Chloe. I'll take her. You can head back with Helen and Cameo."

Just like that conversation is over. I don't know what it is about Reba, but she commands a presence without doing anything at all. There's confidence there. Something I can recognize that Chloe admires. Her chair slides back as she grabs my arm and starts pulling me towards the street. Chloe just sits there shaking her head. The look of relief on her face says more than words could.

"Come on, Auntie. Let's go. I'll be your niece for the day."

Her grip is strong. Doesn't look like I have a choice.

26
THE HUMBLE JOURNEYMAN

"I DON'T KNOW WHY YOU love me, darling." He had been drinking heavily that day. The scent of whiskey danced around him like children to a fire. "I'm not the best man out there."

I knew that a long time ago, but I didn't care. "It doesn't matter. The best is overrated."

His fingers began tracing nonsensical shapes into my back. "If that's true then I've been doing everything backwards. I should stop giving you my best."

I let out a sigh. "That's not what I meant."

He laughed. "Could have fooled me, darling."

"Jameson—"

"You do look gorgeous, you know. Even when you're trying to be modest." And there he was just staring at me. His eyes looked into mine and I knew, without a doubt, that every word he was saying was sincere.

"Stop it." I may have said the words, but I didn't mean them.

He sighed. "No, I will not. Not ever."

***

"You're such a sad person, but I don't think you need to be." Reba walks beside me with both hands in her pockets.

"Oh really?" I shrug. "Why do you care?"

"That's a little harsh. I thought it was obvious."

"What?"

She smiles. "You're complex and I can appreciate that."

I'm not entirely sure what she means. "Complex?"

She pauses. "Very."

"If you say so."

The streets are fairly crowded still. The conversation levels shift from one side of the street to the other. I suppose it is to be expected. Reba shakes her head as a man runs out into the road and narrowly misses getting hit by a couple of kids playing around with a holograph. The man is oblivious. His focus is solely on whatever he is reading on his circuits.

"People are idiots. They're so fascinated with the technical that they forget the simple things which matter." She sighs. "The angle of that impact could have seriously hurt him."

I nod. "But it didn't."

Reba takes a deep breath and turns down a well-lit alleyway. She seems to know where she's going. I haven't been to this part of the city in a long time. These are the blocks leading to the underground. They are probably the closest thing to a slum that this city has.

Without warning the ground starts to shake. Reba and I make brief eye contact before the screaming starts. People are trembling until their legs give out. I don't even realize I'm falling until the ground goes from being under my feet to under my ass. Somehow Reba stays standing though. I'm not sure how she does it. Then, just as fast as it began, everything settles down.

"That wasn't the earth; it was the city." She pauses. "The vibrations were too shallow."

They didn't seem too shallow to me. "The city shakes like that?" I sigh and push myself off the ground. "That's not normal."

She nods. "It has been lately."

"How often does that happen?"

"At least once a week." She starts walking and I follow without hesitation.

It's as if this city is literally falling apart.

One by one the people resume their lucid conversations. We move by them only to catch glimpses of their lives at the present moment. Words float around in no particular order, but the message is clear. People are afraid, and this isn't the kind of fear I am used to seeing. This fear is more subtle; desperate even. That is the worst of all. Anything could happen.

***

"You don't look like you're from around here." His voice was calm with a hint of confidence. Based on the description I knew who he was the moment I saw him. "Just passing through?"

I nodded and took a long drink from the glass in my hand. "Always."

"That sounds lonely." His tone was clear, making it easy to read between the lines.

I shook my head and set the empty glass onto the bar. "I'm not looking for what you're suggesting."

He sighed. "That was a fast transition."

"The conversation was heading that way or am I wrong?"

"No, not at all. You're fun. I can tell just by looking at you."

There was something about him even then that I couldn't stand. The job was going to be hard, I knew that, but this was different. I didn't know it then.

"I think that's enough." I stood. The stool I was sitting on scraped the floor as it slid back. "You shouldn't talk to women like that. It disgusts me."

And I walked without so much as looking back. There was always the possibility that he wouldn't follow. I knew that.

"Wait."

But that wasn't the case there.

I looked over my shoulder, and didn't say a word.

"Let's start over. I'm harmless, really. My name is Jace."

Then I walked out the door. He followed only seconds after.

***

"Carlson, open the door." Reba pounds against

the frame. "We know you're in there."

I pause. "We do?"

She shrugs then hits the door again. "If you don't open it we're going to break it down."

There's only a slight pause before Reba turns to me. The decision is fast, but I don't protest. Instead, I nod and slam my foot into the door just below the handle. The wood cracks and the metal distorts enough to break the latch. It flies open with ease.

It's dark inside. I doubt there is anyone here.

Reba pushes past me and turns on the light in the next room. "Shit."

"What is..." But I stop myself from saying anything else.

The smell of rot and metal fills my lungs the moment I step inside. Down a short hallway, Reba is on her knees looking into the face of a man staring off into absolutely nothing. The blood surrounding the large incision on his left arm has long since dried. Bruises circle his neck just above the collar. The man is dead. There's nothing to gain here.

"His circuits are gone." She stands and takes a couple steps in my direction. "Cut out rather crudely as well."

I shake my head. "This doesn't help us at all. We should go."

She smiles. "This helps us. What are you talking about?"

"The man is dead on the floor. He can't tell us anything."

"No, but I think we just found out how your man is wandering the city without a target on his back." She sighs. "He's probably reprogrammed this guy's circuits for himself."

I pause. "Is that even possible?"

"It is, but it's very expensive. Only a handful of people have the skills to do it." She motions towards the door and puts her hands back in her pockets. "Plus, it's very illegal."

We're making a rather large assumption here, but I can't deny that it makes sense.

The moment Reba steps outside she makes an abrupt stop and both hands leave her pockets. "What are you doing in there?"

"Visiting a friend." She takes a step back inside. Whoever it is follows her motion just enough for me to see the gun.

I flatten myself against the wall and approach slowly.

"Or robbing the place." That voice. It sounds like a man.

I hang back just enough to stay out of sight.

Reba shakes her head. "There is nothing here I need."

I move quickly, place both hands on the gun, and redirect the line of fire. One shot goes off and I feel the barrel get hot, but the pain doesn't register until after I knock the person down. The gun falls, but Reba catches it before it hits the ground.

I pause just enough to really look now. The man on the ground is the engineer from before.

He starts reaching under his jacket, but stops once he sees his gun in Reba's hand.

"Please don't. We're really not here to fight." She doesn't take aim. Instead she releases the power cell and disarms the weapon. "Just stay put and we'll be on our way."

"Wait, do I know you?" He's looking at me now. Our eyes meet, and the recognition comes soon after. He pushes himself off the ground. "You're the one I found in the engine room."

I nod. "Yes, that's right."

For a moment no one says anything. He looks as if he wants to ask me a question, but no words follow. Reba tosses me the gun and leans herself against the wall. "Well I'm leaving. This is getting awkward."

But she doesn't go, at least not right away. Whether she realizes it or not, the scene just got a lot more interesting.

27
THE COWARD'S GUNFIGHT

THERE'S A MAN WHO USED to sit on a bench across from the park I walked by as a kid. Every day when I went to school I would see him hunched over with a book face down on his lap. It was always the same book; might have been the same page as well. I don't know what he was doing or if he was even looking at anything, but he was one of the constant presences I didn't really notice until it disappeared.

His name was Stanley. I only know that because he would mutter it repeatedly under his breath. He wasn't telling it to anyone, just himself. It's important not to forget who we are even when life makes it hard to remember.

"It's my fault." The engineer sits alone at a table while Reba and I make our way to join him. Two doors down, a body slowly decays in a room no one has visited in days. "I should have checked on him. We usually run into each other in the server room."

Reba shakes her head. "It's no one's fault. No one in this room anyway."

I nod. "We're looking for a man named Jason Cross. We think he might have had something to do with this."

He pauses. "Is that the same man you asked me about before?"

"Yes."

"I don't think I can help you."

Reba let's out a long sigh. "Well, then we should probably go."

But there's something hidden between the lines here. I can feel it. There are too many coincidences. A man who doesn't belong doesn't go unnoticed by everyone. It's impossible. There must be someone who knows. I refuse to believe he is a ghost in this city.

"You went to the gathering, right?"

He looks up and nods slowly. "Of course."

I pull out a chair and take a seat. "He was there. On the balcony with the council."

Silence lingers for a moment. He breaks eye contact and closes his eyes. "The presumptuous one? He's the only one I didn't recognize. He's not a member of the council. People have been talking about it."

Talking, unfortunately, does very little in a city like this.

Reba and I make brief eye contact as she makes a shallow motion for the door. There is nothing more to learn here, but something still feels like it's missing. The moment I slide my chair back Reba has her hand on my shoulder. "Wait." She then looks up to the engineer. "I think the ground is going to start shaking again."

The vibrations are small, almost non-existent compared to when we were on the street just a little while ago. I'm surprised she can feel it. I don't. Without prompting the engineer turns, grabs his coat, and gets up from his chair. He looks visibly distraught; the change is subtle, but it is there. Reba doesn't say anything, nor does it look like she plans to. I can never predict what she is going to do. Her actions don't seem to follow any trend.

"Where are you going?" Such a rudimentary question, but I ask it anyway. It's not my business, no, but it is late and the sense of urgency I'm getting from a visibly tired man is enough to concern anyone.

He throws his coat over his shoulder, pulls a device out of his pocket and motions towards the door. "She's right. Pressure is building up in the gauges. Someone needs to release them or they're going to rupture."

"What are you talking about?"

He sighs. "The engines aren't stable. I'm having a hard time rebuilding the release valves. The pressure is causing mass surges in the..." He must see the confusion on my face. I have no idea what he is talking about. "The shaking is my fault. It isn't an earthquake. The whole city is seizing." He pauses before leaving. "Don't worry about locking the door. There's nothing of value in here anyway."

And with those words, he leaves. Doesn't even close the door behind him. Reba continues her inevitable trajectory to the exit and I follow without hesitation. I think we've outstayed our welcome in this place. There's a decaying body in one apartment, and an unstable engineer in the other. I'm not quite sure what to make of all of this. Reba looks to Carlson's apartment one last time before turning away. "At least we have something to go on."

I nod. "Now to see how much it actually helps."

The shaking is still very light, relatively unnoticeable, but it is still there. It isn't until we are about a block away from Helen's that it finally stops. For whatever reason, I can't help but think about that man; the engineer. We've seen each other twice and I haven't even thought to ask what his name was. He's determined on the surface, but his work just floats in the background. I see him, but I don't, and it makes me sad not because I'm faulting myself, but because I'm sure that there is more to him than I know. I just don't think I have time to understand his story.

***

"Teresa, Reba, get in here!" Cameo's voice soars through the restaurant. I think that is the loudest I've ever heard him yell. Reba and I hurry through the empty dining hall to the back rooms. Everyone is gathered in Helen's office. The large monitor is on and standing square in the middle is Jameson.

"Where is this?" Those words come out a little faster than I intend them to.

Chloe looks over and steps away from the table. "Just outside the gates. He wants to talk to someone."

Behind him are several of his best men. I recognize them all. "Is this being broadcast? Can everyone see it?"

"No, we're using the council's secure channel." I don't recognize the voice. That is when I notice him. Standing next to Helen is one of the councilors: Ferdinand. His eyes don't leave the screen. "The people don't know he's banging on our door like an impatient puppy. It would disturb the peace."

I shake my head. "So, is the council just going to leave him out there like that?"

He nods. "That is the plan, until the census results are tallied. He has been asking to see his wife, but he never says her name, so I don't know how to accommodate—"

"It's me he wants to see." There isn't one person in the room that doesn't look away from the monitor for at least a moment. It's Chloe's stare that I feel the most though. She smiles a little, but I'm not sure why.

"Well that solves one mystery." Ferdinand steps away from the monitor and turns towards me. "Would you be willing to speak with him then? I just want to keep the peace. Regardless of the results of the census, I'd like to resolve this without violence." He then turns to Paige. "There's been too much of that here already."

"Of cour—" The moment I go to speak I see Polluck stumble backwards and fall. "What the fuck was that?"

Ferdinand turns back and runs to the controls. "The audio... I don't know where it went."

There's a scramble. Jameson clutches his shoulder. I've seen that look in his eye before; murder. There's nothing else that can describe it.

Two of his men help him up, but he doesn't turn away. He yells, but no one in this room hears him.

Chloe is beside me now. "Aunt Teresa?"

But I don't say anything. There's an ache in my chest. It feels as if it's starting to throb, but I know it isn't really. My senses go into over load. The clicking of the controls, the movement on the screen and Polluck's pained expression is enough. I feel water gathering in the corner of my eye. What comes next is fury that I didn't know I had.

28
THE THINGS WE CANNOT CHANGE

"TERESA, STOP. You need to settle down!" Paige pulls me back from the door.

I fall awkwardly on top of her. The room behind me is in disarray. Cameo pushes himself up from the ground. I may have knocked him out of the way when I turned to leave. I honestly can't remember. The grip around my waist is strong though. It's like I'm being hugged by a bear. Paige holds me still until I stop struggling. That is when I feel the grip lessen and realize just how many people are staring at me.

"Aunt Teresa." Chloe kneels.

I can't look her in the eye. I just don't feel like I should. "That was not fair."

Paige sighs. "Been there, remember?"

Helen shakes her head. "Such a waste. Now no matter what happens there's going to be fighting. He doesn't look like the kind to back down."

"He isn't." I stand and help Paige up as well. "I'm sorry. I shouldn't have–"

"It's fine." She takes a moment to brush herself

off. "Takes a little more than that to hurt me."

"I need to know what this man is capable of." Ferdinand steps past Helen with his circuits flashing. "Our defense resources are rather limited."

I pause. "What do you mean?"

He sighs. "Exactly that. We have the weapons and bots that were installed for basic defense when the city was first built, but only a handful of security. If they breech the walls, then we literally have nowhere to go. We're outnumbered. This isn't Voltza. We aren't ready for war at a moment's notice."

A gang versus a city and the city is outnumbered? All those years no one would go near this place because of just how advanced and intimidating it looked. Seems ironic that a city would bow to a mere handful of men.

I pause as a single thought settles into my mind: he could storm the city. "He's capable of anything."

The room goes silent for a moment. The buzzing of the lights overhead is the only thing louder than our breathing. I can feel Paige's stare the most. She knows what I do. Polluck isn't used to not getting what he wants. His intentions seem genuine, but I know that if I don't go to him then there will be a path of pain carved out in his wake to get to me.

"I need to talk to him." I look only to Ferdinand. "He'll stop if he knows I'm fine."

"I don't think he will." Paige steps between us. "He's just been supremely pissed off. He might pursue this just out of principle."

"He wouldn't–"

"He would. You know that."

Well played, Jace. I have no doubt that this little stalemate we're in now is his doing. Whether I want to admit it or not Paige is right. Polluck won't stop. He doesn't have it in him to demonstrate restraint.

"What about that man you guys are looking for?" Chloe looks to Ferdinand. "He was with the council at the census."

"Jason?" Ferdinand nods. "What about him?"

"He's from outside the city."

The councilor pauses for a moment. "I'd have to disagree with you. His circuits check out. He's been a predominant leader in the underground for several years."

"Reba and I found someone." All eyes are on me now. "He had his circuits cut out."

Reba nods. "Crude butchery. The only reason someone would do that is if they were planning on reprogramming them."

Paige moves towards the window. "That makes a lot of sense actually. All he'd need is a talented doctor."

Ferdinand shakes his head. "Did neither of you hear me? I said he was a prominent leader for years. The incidents can't be related."

Helen nods. "Then why don't you make introductions then? All this guessing from afar doesn't seem to be getting anyone anywhere."

He smiles. "No, it doesn't." He then turns and looks back to us. "Alright, let's drown this theory and get us back to focusing on what's important. There's still an army at our gates and its leader has just been wounded."

"They'll wait for him to recover." I sigh. "He's

the kind of man who likes being there on the front lines. Makes for a better story."

Ferdinand steps back and presses on his circuits. "Meet me at the assembly tomorrow then. I'll arrange for Jason to be there." He looks up to Helen and then to Paige. "You better come as well. I'll redact the bulletin and instate temporary immunity to you for the day. Helen told me what happened, and I don't think this place needs anymore bloodstains. Especially not yours." He then takes Helen's hand and gently places a kiss on her fingers. "Have a good evening, love."

The room goes silent as he walks out.

Helen takes a seat behind her desk and pauses as she looks at the screen. I don't know what is going through her mind, but I do recognize the look on her face. She's strategizing, but I don't know what exactly.

"Are you alright?" Paige is standing directly in front of me now. I hadn't realized that she moved.

"Yes, I'm fine."

She doesn't believe me. I can tell by the look in her eye. I don't even believe myself.

"Can he do that? Just redact an order and allow you to walk around without any problems?" Everyone stares at me as if I am stupid for asking such a question. Reba chuckles to herself, Cameo shakes his head, Paige smiles, and Chloe put her hand on my arm. It looks as if she's going to say something, but stops.

Helen steps forward and sighs. "He's a talented man who can make anything happen."

I shot Jameson once.

Just grazed his arm, but I did it. Saved a man's life as well. There are some things in this world that just cannot be explained. There are days when I hate Polluck. I'm not stupid. I know what he is, but that doesn't change the fact that I still care. Maybe I always will. I don't know. The man really has a death grip on my heart.

29

THE WILTING WALLFLOWER

PEOPLE ARE ALWAYS READY to do the unexpected even if they don't realize it. The Minister is a firm believer in the human question. Is it the nature of the person or the species which defines their actions? I don't think there is an answer to that. People are predictable for the most part, but that doesn't mean we are all cookie cutter perfect with how we act.

The census results are being revealed in a couple of hours. Getting a chance encounter with Jace is easy. I think the stress of this is getting to me. Sleep is hard to come by and when I do sleep it is filled with dreams I don't understand. I am obsessed with this job and it isn't healthy.

"So, you're one of Chloe's aunts? Next to Cameo she's the only one of that group which still has family around, you know?" Ferdinand reaches into his pocket and pulls out a lighter. "She's a lucky girl. Not sure if she knows that though."

Paige smiles and takes a bite of the apple in her hand. "Of course, she does. I think she pities us though. That's why she doesn't move on. She could.

She's about the only of us who can. The city always needs medics."

"She cares too much." Both Ferdinand and Paige are looking at me now. "She's always been too nice, but she isn't an innocent child anymore."

Ferdinand pulls out a cigarette. "She's actually quite brilliant. That's why Helen scouted her." The flame of his lighter flashes for a moment until only a thin trail of smoke remains on the end of the paper tube. "She's going to live for a very long time and help this city more than any of us ever could."

"What do you mean?"

He looks to Paige. "Eleven is a city of art and science..." But he trails off and turns his attention to someone behind us. "Jason, it's good to see you."

Ferdinand moves like we aren't even there. He steps around Paige and offers a hand outstretched to the man approaching us. Our eyes meet for a brief moment. The recognition doesn't seem to be there. Doesn't mean it isn't though.

"Ferdinand, to what do I owe the pleasure?" He's talking differently again; so formal. It doesn't fit him.

"These lovely ladies approached me asking to meet you. They are avid fans of your work with the artistic sciences foundation."

Paige nods. "Charmed. We were wondering if we could take a few minutes of your time to discuss funding opportunities for the Everland Theatre."

Where does she come up with this? The amount of bullshit fermenting around me is getting close to intolerable. I don't think I could ever be in politics.

"Of course. I always have time for inquiries.

Awareness is a powerful tool."

Ferdinand nods. "It is the most powerful."

A moment of silence moves between us. He hasn't looked at me yet. Paige and I are standing right in front of him, but his attention remains almost exclusively on Ferdinand. It's as if he really is meeting us for the first time. Do I have the wrong man? No, he's just crafty and very careful. Jace turns and motions towards a room to the left. The door is wooden, ancient almost in comparison to the others. The three of us follow, but Ferdinand stops just shy of our destination.

He glances over his shoulder for a quick second before stepping in after us. "You three must forgive me, but I think someone is following us."

Jace nods and takes a seat near the window. "Most likely one of my bodyguards. I've taken a few precautions since that maniac appeared outside. Perhaps I'm being a little paranoid. There is, after all, a few literal walls between us, but I'm still not a fan of the situation."

"I don't think there is anyone who is." Paige takes a seat across from him. "Hopefully the census comes back positive for negotiations. We should be able to prove a case for diplomacy here."

"He looks like a dangerous man though." Jace leans forward. "Someone could get hurt and I'd rather not have that on my conscience."

"Why would it be?" I stand back a little and lean against the wall. "It's not like you're the reason he is here."

He nods. "No, I am not, but I take all decisions concerning the well-being of people very seriously.

Call it a sympathy-guilt of sorts. The whole situation is delicate. The people's vote will decide the council's—"

"I think we need to cut the bullshit." My words are harsh, I know they are, but I can't play this game as well as the three of them can. I say what I mean, and I say it directly. This facade sickens me. "What do you think you're playing at, Jace?"

He clears his throat. "I'm sorry I don't know what you're—"

I hit him hard in the jaw. "Finish that sentence. I dare you."

Ferdinand is behind me in seconds. He moves faster than I thought he could. Two men rush through the door, but Jace puts up a hand as if to motion for them to stop. "I assure you that I have no idea where that came from, but hit me again and I'll be pressing charges."

Paige doesn't say anything at first. She pauses for a moment until I know she sees what I do. Just below his left wrist looks like fresh stitches around his circuits. "You look remarkably like someone we know. He's a bit of a scoundrel. Came in with us when we entered the city."

"I don't like false pretenses." Jace is staring directly at Ferdinand. "Least of all from a colleague." He pushes his chair back and continues to hold his jaw. "Disgraceful. Now if you'll excuse me I think all my courtesy is gone for the moment."

He goes to walk by me, but instead he stops abruptly, leans close, and whispers. "Try again next time, Wallflower."

No one else seems to hear it: the break in

character. Paige doesn't react and neither does Ferdinand. I take a deep breath and take three whole seconds to decide what to do next. It isn't really a decision I need to ponder on for too long.

"You son of a whore." Before anyone knows what is happening I've got both hands on his collar and I am pushing him back until he falls on his ass and I end up on top with my fists raised. A loud crack echoes with the first punch. Pain shoots through my hand, but I don't stop. I get a few good shots in before someone pulls me off.

The cuffs go on as the scent of blood fills my lungs. My knuckles are bleeding. The throbbing intensifies as the adrenaline wears off. I can't move my right hand. I probably broke it on his jaw.

"Call me Wallflower again, Jace. Come on. Do it loud enough for everyone to hear."

A man I don't recognize pulls me to my feet while another helps Jace stand. Paige goes to move, but Ferdinand stops her. Where I am going she shouldn't follow. She's already on thin ice in this city. I'm pulled abruptly out the door just as Jace is wiping the blood from his nose. Our eyes meet for a brief second, but that is all.

He still has that smirk.

It's the one thing he cannot hide.

I don't think he's trying to either.

30
THE HARLEQUIN'S CAGE

THE BARS ARE HUMMING almost as loud as the lights. Subsonic waves; they cancel out any sound from the other side of the bars. No one, quite literally, can hear you scream while they are on. A cell like this is supposed to be reserved for very rowdy prisoners who don't know their place. They shouldn't really have it on right now. I haven't said a word since I was dragged off. The only time I utter a sound is when I try to move my hand. It's broken, and I doubt I'll be able to get a doctor to look at it anytime soon.

"That was stupid, Wallflower. Very stupid." Jace walks up to the bars with a rag pressed against his nose. "Now people are going to start asking questions. I was trying to avoid that."

His voice is just how I remember it. Whatever act he's been playing at has fallen to the wayside. There's no doubt that the man across from me is who I have been looking for.

"It wasn't stupid, it was necessary." I stand and walk forward.

He cups a hand around his ear. "I'm sorry. I

can't hear you and I think I like it this way."

"Jace–"

He smiles and lowers the rag. There's nothing but dried blood in its place. "No one will listen to your story that way. Not that they would believe you. You don't call this place home."

For a long moment he doesn't say anything. His footsteps echo just slightly louder than the cage holding me here. There's only the two of us. I think back on Reno and the whole journey up the coast. The Minister suggested that I worry about Jameson, but I realize now that my husband was the least of my concerns. This man in front of me is a con artist, but I still don't know why he dabbles in such deception.

I hate being in the dark.

"When I was fifteen my best friend blew his brains out in the roulette halls. Do you know what he said to me before he stepped through the doors?" He's sitting now on a low stool in the corner of the room. "Mom needs money and I've got to be the man of the house. Tell me, Wallflower, what does that mean?" He sighs. "I'm not your enemy, Teresa. I never was."

There it is. The tone of his voice has changed again.

I shake my head and sit my ass back down on the flat metal bed next to the toilet. "Bullshit."

"I am a Paladin by birthright. My father knew that this city was corrupt from the moment it closed its doors on everyone left behind from the fallout. The other cities are the same. Don't think I have forgotten about them. They will all fall in time, but not before eleven faces its fears." He sighs. "I know what you're thinking, but you're wrong. What I am doing is the right thing. Jameson Polluck is the man who is going to educate the people who look down on us like ants."

"No, Polluck is going to kill them all."

He's not even looking at me. "It's for the greater good. Besides..." He pauses briefly. "When everything looks hopeless and the carnage is at its end I'll kill the villain. Whoever is left will follow me because I'll be the hero. People love heroes."

The ground beneath us begins to shake. I am startled just like I was the first time this happened. Jace; however, doesn't seem concerned in the slightest. If anything, he seems oblivious to what's happening.

"We've been planning this for a long time, Wallflower. The knights never died when my father passed on. They just got smarter when it came to conducting business." The shaking settles as Jace stands and turns towards the door. "I know all about you. I have for some time. You're brash and predictable, but you only have one more part to play in all this and then you can move on like you always do. Stay here, will you? Can you do that for me?"

I don't say anything.

He smiles. "That's a good girl."

The shaking starts again, but it's milder this time. Just as before, Jace doesn't seem to notice. He pauses, only for a moment, then leaves out the door he entered. I stare ahead with little to think about, but the throbbing of my hand. There's nothing to do for now, but wait this out.

I hate it.
I really do.

***

"Hey, wake up!" The voice echoes but I barely hear it. I'm still half asleep when a man flies into the bars and shorts out the sub-sonic emitter. It takes a moment for my eyes to adjust, but there is a definite silhouette standing at the door.

"Paige?" No, scratch that. There are two people at the door. "Chloe?"

Neither one of them respond right away. A distinct metal click pings off the cage. Chloe forces the door open and hurries inside. "Aunt Teresa, are you alright?"

Honestly, I'm not sure. "I've been better." I go to push off the bed, but I forget, for a moment, that my hand is broken.

I wince.

Chloe reaches into the kit around her shoulder.

Another guard bursts into the room rifle in hand. Paige moves faster than I have ever seen her before. She kicks out his left knee while diverting the line of fire up. Several bullets burst into the ceiling as he falls. Another kick to the abdomen and he lets go of the rifle.

Two more shots erupt.

He stops moving.

Paige tosses the gun aside. "We've got to go."

Footsteps echo. I know I'm not the only one who hears it. The three of us make our way down the hall with Paige obviously in the lead. I don't recognize this place. It bothers me that I have no clue where I am.

"Polluck has started attacking the wall. The census doesn't matter anymore. This place is going to be a battlefield." Paige turns left and continues leading us down the hall. "We're springing you out, so you can calm him down."

I sigh. "Is that the only reason?"

Chloe shakes her head. "Of course not."

The door bursts open at the end of the hall. Paige draws the gun off her hip and fires instinctively. "Reba and Cameo are holding the lobby. We need to get up to them."

In all truth it might be impossible to calm Jameson down. The man isn't used to not getting his own way and when he's on a rampage there's almost nothing that can stop him.

Paige kicks in a door leading to a rather windy flight of stairs. I don't ask why we aren't taking the elevator.

"Don't move! Put your hands on the wall!" A man stands on the landing with a rifle aimed at the door. I pull Chloe back towards cover, but Paige just keeps charging forward.

Two shots and a large thud ring through the air.

"Come on, let's go!" We look back in and see the man face down sprawled across several stairs. "Stop staring and come on." Paige is ruthless. She moves quickly and confidently forward.

Bullets fly at her, but it's as if she's throwing them right back. Chloe and I find ourselves stepping over the bodies she leaves behind. When we finally reach the top floor she's out of bullets. Two men stand between us and the exit. She doesn't hesitate, not in the slightest. It's terrifying.

She reaches under the back of her shirt and for a moment I see the sheath of a knife. A man fires but she's already crouched and charging into him. His gun falls down several steps as she turns to the other guard. Her blade finds its way into his throat, but not before a handgun erupts.

The other guard recovered quickly.

For the first time since this climb began Paige stops. The red pouring from her arm drips down to her fingertips. The gun aimed at her head is only seconds from going off again.

Bang.

The guard falls. Chloe stands with the fallen rifle in her hands.

"Frick, that was close."

I don't have time to say anything. Chloe pulls me up the stairs as Paige opens the door for us. What we see is nothing short of frightening.

"You're late. Helen isn't going to be happy." Reba tosses Paige a small tourniquet. "You're bleeding all over the place."

Cameo shrugs and pushes a new magazine into his weapon. "Doesn't matter. We're leaving anyway."

The bodies are what amaze me. I can see the metal enhancements and broken tubing. At least three of the dead were fully trained Paladins.

"Is she out the front or the back?" Paige throws the tourniquet aside.

I don't hear anything else. This whole lobby

looks like a war zone and here I am standing with the victors. I can't help, but stare at Chloe as she pulls me along. These people she's with; I don't know what it is they were trained for, but it wasn't to combat this world. Paige alone is evidence of that.

My steps are heavy.

Are these what commanders really are?

I don't know.

I just don't.

31
THE NOBILITY OF KNIGHTS

"IT'S THAT ENGINEER. He keeps pushing the machinery too hard. The city is going to break apart." Paige shakes her head. "People are starting to get hurt."

I'd believe that. The shaking has gotten more and more violent with each passing hour. Though her tone is less than heartless. I picked it up, and believe me I'm not the only one.

"Maybe we should help him. It might give us an alternative to fighting a skirmish we can't win." Reba sits with her arms crossed and a book in her lap. "Are you OK with that though?" Her eyes are fixed on Paige and no one else. "We could do it. All four of us are smart enough."

And suddenly it feels as if the room drops a couple of degrees.

Paige doesn't say a word. No one does. At least, not for a moment.

"I think at this point in time it doesn't matter what Paige is OK with. If the city flies again then maybe we can avoid an unnecessary fight that we aren't prepared for." Ferdinand enters the room with Helen close behind. "That was reckless, Teresa. A waste of resources, an extensive cover story, and now you've exposed one of this city's greatest secrets to a society that never needed to know about it."

"Me?" I shake my head. "I didn't ask to be rescued."

He nods. "No, but you must have known that Chloe wasn't going to accept you being left behind."

The thought hadn't occurred to me at all. I turn and look at Chloe, but she makes no attempt to establish eye contact. "Look—"

"No, you look. This is what the moments before a full-scale war look like. You've passed by wars before. I'm sure you understand that the best thing here and now is for this city to return to where it belongs." And so here, at this moment, Ferdinand's inner politician comes out in full stride.

I step around the table towards him. "If that is how you feel why haven't you already done it?"

"Simple." Helen moves around Ferdinand. "St. Joseph's has always followed a democratic republic style government. We vote here. Not everyone wants to go back."

"And keeping your doors shut to the outside world was a better option?"

"It's what was voted."

"So now, after all this time you're going to make a choice for them? Doesn't sound like much of a democracy. If anything, it sounds like a very large and convenient excuse."

Ferdinand shakes his head. "We don't really have a choice now do we?"

Cameo keeps his head down with Chloe. Neither one of them say anything in response. Paige and Reba watch the conversation in anticipation. I don't know what I am doing. Decisions like these are above me. I just want to go back to doing my job the only way I know how. I won't ever be breaking my own rules again. Things just get too complicated.

"And what about Jace?"

The question sits for a moment.

"He's a con man. I will admit that I think I was in denial, but everything checked out on the surface." He pauses for a moment. "You have my apologies on that one."

Without warning a large bang echoes through the air. All of us react in different ways. I'm on the ground within seconds. Shadows of the past play through my mind. Helen runs towards her computer. Another bang erupts. Then two more after that.

"It's Polluck. He's firing bloody cannons."

I pause just long enough to hear the vibration of metal footsteps coming towards us. We all hear it. I'm reaching for something, anything I can use as a weapon. Only one thing makes a noise like those steps. This right here is the definition of being caught in the middle.

"Some fights are necessary and the people who stop them are just delaying the inevitable." The voice carries past the steps. There are multiple sets. Jace? It almost sounds like him.

"Paladins."

Those with weapons reach for them. I grab Chloe and pull her down with me. She has a gun and she intends to use it, but I don't want her to. The steps get gradually louder until I see the unmistakable metal suits emerge through the door. The men inside contort just enough to twist through the small opening, but not before brushing against the frame and cracking the wall.

Helen slowly reaches for something under her desk.

"This little place is quite the powerful establishment." The man in the middle pauses for a moment to remove his helmet. "There are more sub-levels here than surface ones. Simply brilliant." He takes a moment to scan the room before settling on Helen. "My name is Jason Cross. You must be the leader of this little outfit. Helen, was it?" Ferdinand makes a move, but one of the other men grabs his shoulder and pushes him to his knees. "Now, councilor, please don't. I want to try and have at least one of you survive this. Don't be like your colleagues. You're smarter than that."

"That's my name."

Jace turns his attention back to Helen. "Splendid. I was hoping we could have a conversation."

She nods. "Looks like I don't have a choice. You've already arrived and let yourself in. How rude."

He bows slightly. "My apologies, but under the circumstances it seemed like the best thing to do."

Helen slides her chair back and stands with a look of boredom on her face. "So, what is it that you wanted to talk about? You're hardly in the attire for a talk."

"An alliance. I hear you're the real one who

runs this city." He pauses then looks to each of us. "And you have quite a few resources that could be very helpful in the coming days. There's a mad man outside and somehow I don't think just talking to him will be enough." He stares right at me as he says it. "That and I'm sure you've already spoken to Teresa. I'm not your enemy. I just want to change the system."

She pauses. "The system is beyond flawed. It is unfair and ruthless to outsiders."

He smiles. "I'm glad that you—"

"But I hardly think this is the way to change it."

"Then I need to show you—"

"Show me what?" She steps around the desk. "You're so aggressive. Just like Sergio was. He had ideas too, but his problem was that he was too much of a military man. Sometimes you can end a fight with a conversation, but unless you try first you are no different than the cruel world you think you're trying to change."

"The world doesn't listen."

She nods. "That is because more than a few people are just too stupid to care."

He steps forward. "This seems like our conversation is going nowhere. I came here to reach an accord. Is that at all possible?"

For a long moment Helen doesn't say anything. I can tell she's thinking about it. All of us are just members of the audience watching the events unfold. The other man's grip on Ferdinand's shoulder tightens.

A low grunt travels through the air before Helen looks up and smiles. "Fuck no." Then, just as those words leave her mouth she reaches behind her back and draws an energy pistol. The flash of light is so strong that I don't think anyone is able to look at it without turning away right after.

Jace falls. His metal suit thumps onto the ground. The hole in his chest is the size of a soccer ball and it didn't stop with him. The men standing directly behind him are on their knees clenching different parts of their bodies. The beam went straight through and then some. Only the man holding Ferdinand remains standing.

"I think all of you should go." And they do, but not before taking a good long look at the man who called himself Jason Cross.

32
THE SHADOW BEFORE
THE SUNSET

THERE ARE MANY REASONS why energy weapons have long since been outlawed. This scene right here is one of them. Helen is next to Ferdinand within seconds. Neither one of them exchange words. They don't need to. Actions were quite clear on this one.

"Holy shit, Helen." Cameo stands up and takes in the scene. "Don't you think that could have been handled a little better?"

Helen shakes her head. "He pissed me off, Cam."

Ferdinand pushes himself up and grabs his own shoulder. "I don't think I can handle any more of this."

Helen nods. "You won't have to. We all know what we need to do to end this lapse into stupidity."

Reba starts walking toward the door. "You don't have to tell us twice, HB. I'll find the engineer. I'm just about ready for things to get back to normal."

She leaves just as Cameo gathers himself. "I'll go talk to my brother. He should be able to help a little."

Despite all this, Chloe still looks only at me. The conversations carry on, but I don't hear them. "Are you OK?"

She looks at me as if she knows something I don't. "Yeah."

"Are you sure?"

I smile. "You don't believe me?"

"No." She sighs. "Not really."

Helen falls backwards as the ground shakes again. The pictures on the wall buckle for a few seconds before they plummet off the hooks holding them in place. Cameo races out the door as I grab Chloe and pull her behind me. We're outside in seconds, but the sight in front of us looks similar to cities I've seen before.

The smell of fire lingers in the distance. Debris litters the streets and people cower frantically in the open. Where do you go when the ground doesn't want to hold you up anymore? This city isn't built like a planet. Shaking, for any reason, isn't natural and with or without the screams, the people are terrified. I'm not there yet, but I am pretty close.

Explosions sound off in the distance.

A child whimpers somewhere to the left.

Polluck hasn't stopped.

He won't either.

"This is ridiculous. The walls won't hold." Chloe pulls away from me and turns back to the restaurant. "I need to get my bag. People could be hurt."

I shake my head. "We need to stay away from buildings. They're not stable."

"It doesn't matter." She runs and doesn't so much as look back.

Helen and Ferdinand hurry out just as she goes back in. "What is she doing?"

But I don't say anything. I can't. Something flies and bursts through the roof. I take one step, maybe two, as the building collapses. "Chloe!"

The shaking ceases for a moment and silence settles the city for a few seconds.

"Get back." Helen pulls my shoulder hard enough to knock me off my feet. More projectiles fall. Jameson is using the launchers.

"Get out of my way!" I try to get up, but Ferdinand pushes me back down.

"We need to get you to him now before he tears the city apart."

"Like hell you do." The explosions are overwhelming. I feel like a child trapped between a corner and something I really don't want to do. "Get out of my..." But I don't finish the sentence. A piece of debris flies back and I see Paige helping Chloe through one of the collapsed walls.

"Don't be selfish. None of us have that luxury. We all have jobs to do here which will ensure we all survive."

I pause. "No, I don't think you understand. If something happened to her then it doesn't matter. It simply doesn't matter. Nothing does."

Their looks are clear.

Judgment.

I've seen it before, but that is alright because at this moment, as Paige walks towards me, I have nothing but respect. Our eyes meet for a second; no more, no less. She grabs hold of my arm and pulls me towards the gates. Chloe only looks to Helen.

It's as if I don't exist. Perhaps I am being selfish. I won't say sorry for that. The city needs more than empty apologies.

**

The air has gotten colder. The smell of rain lingers in the distance. Paige and I sprint through the streets like we're running through a minefield. We don't know when the next bit of debris will fall or if we'll get struck by it, but that seems to be the way the game goes. We're traveling through a place where the environment could very well be our downfall. I don't want to die this way. It feels too convenient.

Just as we turn the corner Paige stumbles over a small baseball sized crater. She recovers quickly, but not without a moment of wincing.

"You going to make it?"

She nods. "Yeah, I've just been pushing the limits of my body lately. I can feel it starting to rebel."

When we finally reach our destination, the building and its exterior are barely recognizable. We hop in through a hole in the wall and continue down the corridor leading to the quarantine section. There's nobody here. I suppose I should have expected that.

"The gate controls are down that way, right?"

I pause. "I have no idea."

"Frick." She sighs. "Only one way to find out then."

I find myself standing at the grand door as Paige enters one of the adjacent rooms. A few moments pass before I hear the rough squeal of the gears shifting within the walls. The explosions echo louder than when we were in the heart of the city.

"Jameson!" I can see him across the way. He turns just as the door fully opens and locks into place.

He's nothing but a dot in the distance; a distinct one. I doubt he heard me call his name, but it doesn't matter. The launchers are powered down as several men hurry towards the new opening. Polluck is coming, but not nearly as fast as I thought he would.

"Whoa, he does not look happy." Paige stands just a few feet behind me. "Maybe this wasn't such a good idea."

I shrug. "There's no going back now."

The way he moves tells me more than most people will ever know. Each step he takes commands notoriety. Within seconds I'm looking straight down the barrels of several rifles. No one takes a step onto the ramp. I can see the caution in their eyes. Paige moves back a little.

"Jameson."

He can hear me now. The light gray combat armor clanks as he walks. "There you are." He pauses. "Did he hurt you, darling?" His eyes are stuck on the makeshift cast around my wrist.

"No."

Suddenly, a violent pulse shifts from the ground up. The shaking starts again, and I find myself face down on the ramp with the taste of blood filling my mouth. Jameson moves, but to my surprise, so does the ground.

Paige stumbles backwards. "Holy frick. They did it."

I watch as the city begins a slow lift off and the distance between Jameson and I grow by the foot. He reaches for the ramp, but the edge slips out of his hand.

"No." I look up as he turns and shouts towards the launchers.

He won't stop.

He never will.

I realize that at this moment a choice has presented itself. I know my husband. He's not going to let me go and anymore damage might just drop the city back to earth. The impact, however small it might be, could still hurt a lot of people.

"I'm going down." I push myself to stand.

"What?" Paige calls out, but I'm already at the edge of the ramp. Thoughts of Chloe flood my mind and they become the only reason I don't jump right away. "Teresa!" Paige calls out to me, but I don't look back.

"I'm going to deal with this and then come back for her." I'm trembling as the ground slowly grows farther away.

"Wait—"

If she said anything else, I couldn't hear it.

"Teresa!" Jameson's voice echoes as I jump.

In this moment there is only silence until my boots crush the distorted gravel sprinkling the earth. My knees give out and I find myself flat on my back looking up as the city rises.

"Teresa!" Jameson is over me in what feels like an instant. He pulls me up and holds me tight as I take my first few shallow breaths in his arms. His hands are rough.

I can't look at him right away. Being this close feels wrong. "You can stop now. Please don't hurt them."

He holds me tighter. "Darling..."

I just watch as the city rises farther and farther away until it is nothing but a patch in the sky. Something wet hits my face and I look up to see Jameson with a small transparent streak parting the dirt on his cheek. For the first time since that door opened we make eye contact. Real, uninterrupted, eye contact.

I think of Chloe and of how many times Paige may have yelled my name before it was completely muffled in the distance. Jameson and I stare at each other just waiting for the other person to make their move, but neither of us do. Between us, there is only silence. Sometimes that is much more powerful than any spoken word.

I won't be anyone's darling anymore...

~TJL~

WHAT'S NEXT?

INTRODUCING

If you enjoyed VIOLENT SKIES,
be on the lookout for

URBAN HEROES

1

THE RUSSIAN REVOLVER

IF SOMEONE ASKED ME what the most terrifying sound was, I would say the spinning clicks of a metal cylinder. The room is quiet. I sit on a cold chair with both hands palm down on a rusty metal table. A man sits across from me. Sweat drips down his forehead as he reaches for the revolver that lay between us. Does he think I can't see his hand shaking? He isn't the only one who's afraid.

I watch as he inches the end of the barrel to his temple and closes his eyes. After a deep breath, he pulls the trigger. I let out a sigh when the only sound I hear is an empty click.

"Frick yeah. Would have been a shame to go out just like that." His cocky demeanour returns the moment he sets the revolver back onto the table. "You know, girly, I won't blame you for backing out. Hell, I would with the odds dropping. I'd rather not see your brains splattered against that wall. I promise I won't laugh at you."

"You aren't the smartest, are you? The odds don't drop unless you forget to spin the cylinder." I pick up the gun and run my palm against the barrel. This revolver has been dropped a few times. There are a few shallow nicks along every groove. "Or maybe that increases the odds." The gun clicks as the cylinder spins. "You look like you're afraid. It's nothing to be ashamed about."

He leans forward. "Come now, girly–"

"Don't call me girly."

He laughs and points to the cameras across the room. "I know people like you. You're a mean one. You think you're so smart. You think that this place is beneath you. News flash, girly, those fuckers don't give two shits about which one of us gets out of this room. It's all about the money. So let's put on a decent show."

I raise the gun and pull the trigger. Nothing, just an empty click. "I'm not an entertainer." I slide the gun across the table. "Go."

"No, but I bet you're an arrogant bitch. You sit like it, anyway." He picks up the revolver. "Too bad you and I didn't meet outside. I could've shown you a good time."

Another click and the revolver slides over to me. "I really doubt it."

"Well, it would've been good for one of us at least, and that's all that would matter."

I pull the trigger then pass the gun. "So vulgar."

Fear makes confidence sound authentic when it shouldn't. This man is a deadbeat. His eyes are bloodshot and his nails are cracked and scabbed over like someone cut them off with a laser; wouldn't surprise me if that were the case. He terrifies me, but this isn't the place to show that. Underneath the table, I find myself gripping the edges of my seat.

He shifts forward. His chair squeaks. "You have a name?"

I look him right in the eye. "You're not supposed to ask that question."

He puts the revolver to his head. "Quit being a goody-goody. I'm just trying to lighten the mood a little. After all, one of us ain't getting—"

Gunshot.

It happens just like that. I close my eyes. Something wet slides down the side of my neck. I try not to think about it. Blood splatter covers the wall, and I'm left wiping stray drops of red from my cheek. Couldn't even shoot himself straight. His body slumps forward onto the table. I slide my chair back to avoid getting caught up in more of the mess. I can feel my breathing increase. I force myself to calm down.

Keep it together, Calista. You're almost out of this rathole.

The lock on the door behind me shifts out of place. A large man stands with his arms crossed. "Congratulations."

I stand and hurry out. The air is cooler, and the smell of blood is less potent. My arm brushes against his, leaving a distinct red smear on the fabric of his gray suit. He doesn't seem to notice. "You have a towel or something?"

"No." His demeanor is all business.

It's always like this. I don't know why I keep asking. I pull off the shirt I'm wearing and start wiping away as much of the blood as I can. I know he's watching. I can feel it. It doesn't matter.

The moment I look up, I see how he's looking at me, inspecting my attire. "Touch me and I'll cut your hand off."

He turns away. "Now there's that feisty spirit. That's why the viewers love you, but you were fairly tame today. It's a shame. The payout is smaller."

I've seen that look before. "Do I see you or Gregov about the money?"

He reaches into his pocket and pulls out a thick brown envelope. "I have it here." I grab the end, but he doesn't let go. "As much as I'm sure people love watching a good game of Russian Roulette, this is your seventh time winning. Your luck is bound to run out eventually, and forgive me if I'm wrong, but it just doesn't look like your heart is in this anymore."

My heart was never in this.

I pull the envelope from his fingers. "You let me worry about that."

He nods. "I'm not complaining. I rather enjoy having a familiar face around here. I just don't want to have to answer to the Maverick if his daughter ends up shooting her own brains out."

Right there, the conversation halts. He recognizes my shift in posture and takes a step backwards. I turn away and gather up my jacket from the hook on the wall. "I think you have me mistaken for someone else."

"I meant no offense. The broadcasts only go to the lower city, and no one there—"

I tuck the envelope in my jacket. "I said, you must have me mistaken for someone else."

He raises his hands defensively "Look I only know because I've been up there before. The people down here are nothing. Expendable." I pull out a pair of knuckles and carefully slip them over my fingers. "Now that I think about it, you can't be her. She wouldn't be caught dead in these slums."

At least the man can take a hint. "You should watch what you say. You're going to get yourself killed."

His eyes follow me to the door. We don't exchange any more words; we don't need to. He knows that I come here because the money is quick and easy, nothing more. The moment I step into the elevator, we are both in the worlds we were meant to live in. This industry of crude entertainment doesn't suit me, but I won't deny that it has served its purpose.

The cold air punches me hard as I step out into the streets. The smell is different out here. It's even more vile than inside. I hurry around the corner and lean against the same dumpster I visit after every round. The contents of my stomach splash against the pavement.

I won't be coming back.

I don't need to.

The money only needs to keep us afloat for a little while longer anyway.

WANT TO READ MORE?

VISIT *MECHAPANDAPUBLISHING.COM* FOR
ACCESS TO THE FULL CATALOGUE

AND

STAY UP TO DATE WITH NEW RELEASES BY
SUBSCRIBING TO OUR NEWSLETTER AT

*MECHAPANDAPUBLISHING.COM/
SUBSCRIBE/*

ABOUT THE AUTHOR

T.J. Lockwood was born somewhere along the west coast of Canada during a relatively mild summer in comparison to the ones which followed. An avid practitioner of the Martial Arts, she is always up for a friendly match or two when time permits. Her writing has, and always will, dive head first through the many portals of Science Fiction. She lives in Vancouver and enjoys the frequently rainy days common in the lower mainland. The honey badger is her spirit animal.

TJLOCKWOOD.WORDPRESS.COM

@TJLwriting

THANK YOU FOR READING.